The Apprenticeship of Lucas Whitaker

Also by Cynthia DeFelice

The Apprenticeship of

Lucas Whitaker

Cynthia DeFelice

SQUARE
FISH

Farrar Straus Giroux   New York

**SQUARE
FISH**

An Imprint of Macmillan

THE APPRENTICESHIP OF LUCAS WHITAKER.
Copyright © 1996 by Cynthia C. DeFelice.
All rights reserved. Printed in the United States of America by
R. R. Donnelley & Sons Company, Harrisonburg, Virginia. For information, address
Square Fish, 175 Fifth Avenue, New York, NY 10010.

Square Fish and the Square Fish logo are trademarks of Macmillan and
are used by Farrar Straus Giroux under license from Macmillan.

Library of Congress Cataloging-in-Publication Data
DeFelice, Cynthia C.
The apprenticeship of Lucas Whitaker / Cynthia C. DeFelice.
p. cm.
Summary: After his family dies of consumption in 1849, twelve-year-
old Lucas becomes a doctor's apprentice.
ISBN 978-0-374-40014-9
[1. Apprentices—Fiction. 2. Orphans—Fiction. 3. Physicians—
Fiction. 4. Medicine—History—Fiction.] I. Title.
PZ7.D3597Ap 1995   [Fic]—dc20   95-26728

Originally published in the United States by Farrar Straus Giroux
First Square Fish Edition: December 2011
Square Fish logo designed by Filomena Tuosto
mackids.com

10 9 8 7 6

AR: 5.2 / F&P: U / LEXILE: 830L

For Leslee Rogath and Nancy Stein—
friends far away,
but close to my heart

The macabre "cure" for consumption, now called tuberculosis, described in this story was practiced in rural New England in the nineteenth century. How we came to know it is a story in itself . . .

In 1990, in Griswold, Connecticut, two boys were sliding down the steep sides of an open gravel pit when they noticed, to their horror, that rolling along with them down the hill were two human skulls. Thinking that perhaps they had come upon evidence of a recent double murder, the boys contacted the police. The medical examiner quickly determined that the skulls were more than fifty years old, which meant that, by law, the remains had to be examined for possible historical significance.

Nicholas Bellantoni, archaeologist for the state of Connecticut, discovered that the skulls had come from an abandoned colonial cemetery on the upper rim of the gravel pit. One of the graves, marked with the initials "JB," had been opened after burial, and the bones had clearly been rearranged in a skull and crossbones pattern. Furthermore, JB's skeleton revealed the scarring of tuberculosis.

Bellantoni worked with Paul Sledzik, curator of the anatomical collection at the National Museum of Health and Medicine, and Michael Bell, anthropologist and folklorist with the Rhode Island Heritage Commission. Using skeletal remains from other sites, along with written accounts found throughout New England, they pieced together evidence of a nineteenth-century folk medical practice based on a belief in what anthropologists call vampirism. In many movies, vampires are shown to suck the blood of their victims, but they may also prey upon the living in other ways.

I'd like to thank Nicholas Bellantoni, Paul Sledzik, and Michael Bell for sharing their findings with me, especially Nick Bellantoni, who gave so generously of his time and enthusiasm. Also, my heartfelt gratitude goes to Bird Stasz, who traveled back to the imaginary town of Southwick with me on many a long walk, to discuss the life and times of Lucas Whitaker.

The Apprenticeship of Lucas Whitaker

One

The Connecticut countryside, 1849

The grave was dug. Carefully, Lucas Whitaker hammered small metal tacks into the top of the coffin lid to form his mother's initials: H.W., for Hannah Whitaker. Then he stood up to straighten his tired back. All that was left was to lower the pine box into the cold, hard ground and cover it with dirt.

But Lucas didn't move. He stared blindly at the double line of grave markers in the little family burial ground. There were the graves of two infants, his brother and sister, each of whom had died so soon after birth that Lucas could scarcely remember anything about them except the sight of their tiny, red fists waving in the air and the sound of their feeble crying. Their graves were so small that the fieldstones stuck in the ground to mark their heads and feet were no farther apart than the length of Lucas's arm.

Next were the stones marking the place where Lucas's Uncle Asa was buried. Asa had died of consumption two years before. Soon after, Lucas's sister Lizy, just four years old, had fallen to the same dread disease.

When they'd buried Lizy, Lucas and his father had worked together in stunned silence, afraid to think about, much less speak about, the mysterious way in which the sickness could sweep through a household, taking one family member after another.

That night Lucas's mother had clasped him to her, weeping. "How long shall I be allowed to keep you?" she'd whispered.

But the next to be afflicted had not been Lucas. He shuddered as he remembered the way the large, powerful man who had been his father had turned slowly into a thin, pale stranger, too weak to stand. Until at last Lucas, working alone on a hot August day, tears mingling with the sweat of his labor, had buried his father, too.

Now, standing on the rocky hillside by his mother's grave, with the raw wind of late February tearing at his hair and clothing, Lucas felt nothing but a dull, gray weariness. Since the death of his father and Asa, it had taken every bit of strength he had just to make it from day to day. He'd learned to push his sorrow deep inside somewhere in order to get on with the hard work that was always waiting to be done on the farm.

4

When his mother's cheeks grew first flushed and red, then gray and gaunt, when she began to be taken by fits of coughing that left her clutching her chest in pain, Lucas gave up trying to keep the farm going. He spent his days by his mother's bedside, watching her waste away just as Lizy, and Pa, and Asa had done. He coaxed her to take spoonsful of tea and wheat porridge. Holding her thin shoulders as her body was racked with coughing, he thought helplessly that it was as if something—or someone—were draining the very life from her.

Desperately, he tried the only remedy he knew, filling a pipe with dried cow dung and begging his mother to smoke it. The coughing only grew worse.

One day, a neighbor by the name of Oliver Rood rode out to the farm and offered to take care of the animals. "I hear your mother's real bad sick, Lucas. I'll take the creatures off your hands for the present, and come back in a few days to see how you're getting on."

"I'd be grateful to you, sir," said Lucas.

Finally, the time came when he could no longer pretend that his mother would live. There was nothing to do but stay by her until death came. When she was gone, he felt something rise in his throat, a mixture of terror and anger and grief so strong that he was afraid to give voice to it.

Summoning all the strength of his will, he pushed the feeling down and down . . . until he'd felt the way he did now, his insides as numb and cold as the rough red hands that grasped the shovel.

Quickly, he finished the job. Then, opening his mother's Bible, he tried to read, but the words sounded stiff and hollow and held no comfort. He closed the book. There were people who had told him to accept the deaths in his family as "God's will." But, hard as Lucas tried, he couldn't understand why God would want such things to happen.

Other folks had told him disease was the work of the devil. Still others believed it was witches who caused illness. He shook his head, baffled by it all. People got sick. They died. That he knew.

There were no friends or family to join him in mourning. The closest neighbors, the Hapgoods, had sold their farm and gone west, where the land was supposed to be cheap and plentiful. Lucas hadn't carried word to the Roods, or to any others. Their farms were far away. They had their own work and their own problems.

Lucas was alone.

Two

Lucas stood inside the doorway of the cold, quiet, empty house. Hours passed, or maybe minutes; he was indifferent to the passing of time. He, too, felt still and cold and empty.

Vaguely, he became aware of the sound of approaching hoofbeats, followed by loud knocking at the door.

"Lucas? You there? Anybody home?"

Dully, Lucas walked to the door and opened it. Oliver Rood was standing on the granite step with a kettle in his hands.

"Hello, Lucas. Mrs. Rood sent me over with some soup. You and your mama have to keep your strength up, and Mary claims this is just the thing. How is Hannah faring, son?"

"She—" Lucas tried to tell Mr. Rood what had happened, but the words got caught in his throat. He swallowed and looked down at the rough plank flooring without answering.

"Still doing poorly, eh?" said Mr. Rood sympathetically. "Well, Lucas, the fact is, the soup isn't the only reason for my visit. May I come in?"

They were standing at the door, with the winter wind blowing into the house. Some part of Lucas's mind knew that it was rude to keep a guest standing at the door, but he seemed to be having difficulty summoning even the most common courtesy. He stepped back, allowing Mr. Rood to enter.

After closing the door and setting the kettle on the table, Mr. Rood cleared his throat and said, "Lucas, you know what we've been going through these past months, with the consumption taking first Mercy, then Frances and Gurdon and Phoebe."

Lucas nodded.

"Then Enoch came down sick, you know. But we cured him."

Lucas stared, uncomprehending, at his neighbor.

"Mrs. Rood heard tell of the remedy while visiting her kinfolk in Rhode Island."

Lucas listened, first with puzzlement, then with fascinated horror, as Oliver Rood explained. "What Mrs. Rood learned is that the first in the family to die is sometimes, in truth, undead."

"Undead?" Lucas repeated.

"Yes," said Mr. Rood. "And, this being so, that person will then rise up from the grave and return to commit mischief on the living."

"Wh-what kind of mischief?" Lucas asked.

Mr. Rood shifted uncomfortably. "They say he—or she—being desirous of sustenance, comes back to feed upon the living. To drain the very life from others in order to live himself."

An image of Mama, slowly wasting away, filled Lucas's mind. It was followed by the memory of his Uncle Asa, who had been the first to die. In Lucas's imagination, Asa rose from his grave and returned to the house, to take first Lizy, then Pa, then Mama—but no! Asa wouldn't hurt Mama. She was his sister! Quickly, Lucas shook his head to make the terrible thoughts go away.

Mr. Rood seemed to know what was in Lucas's mind. "It struck me as peculiar at first. Ghoulish, even. But, Lucas, Mrs. Rood heard the accounts herself. Two families who were afflicted in the way ours was, and yours, did unearth the body of the first dead. They did as they'd been told to put the mischievous one to rest, thereby saving the remaining family members from sickness and death."

Mr. Rood went on. "Persuaded by these successes, we dug up the coffin of daughter Mercy. She was the first to die, you see."

Lucas shivered. Mr. Rood stared piercingly at him.

9

"Enoch was bad sick, Lucas, and going fast. You understand, we were willing to try—anything—by then."

"Yes," said Lucas. And he did understand. He remembered, too well, the helpless feeling of watching someone slip away, and the desire to do something, anything, to stop the course of the disease.

"Daughter Mercy *did live* in the grave, Lucas. We saw the signs."

"What signs?" Lucas whispered.

Mr. Rood spoke slowly, his eyes intent. "I shall never forget it as long as I live: there, on the face of she who had for long weeks been the tenant of a grave, I saw the look of youthful health. Her body was fresh, her cheeks full and dimpled, her hair as rich and curly as it had been in life. Her eye had barely lost its brilliancy. Why, her fingernails had grown!"

Mr. Rood shook his head at the memory. "We had been told to look for these things, Lucas. And to discover if there was fresh, living blood. And, by God, round about her mouth, there was."

For a moment Lucas and Mr. Rood stared at each other in silence, Mr. Rood remembering what he had seen, Lucas trying to take in what he had heard.

"So we did as we'd been instructed. We put Mercy to rest. And now the sickness has stopped. Enoch is cured!"

"I'm glad," Lucas managed to say. Mr. Rood's son Enoch was a year older than Lucas, and the two boys

10

got on well when their families helped each other at haying time.

"Have you considered," Mr. Rood went on, "that your Uncle Asa might be the mischievous one?"

"Asa? I—no," said Lucas.

"He was the first to die, wasn't he?"

"Yes, but—"

"He's likely the one, then. He made the others sick and now he's bothering Hannah."

But Asa was dead! thought Lucas.

Mr. Rood continued speaking. "It might not be too late to save your mother, son. Fact is, I stopped by two days ago to tell you about this. I knocked and hollered, but I couldn't rouse anyone."

Lucas recalled, as if through a fog, sitting by his mother's bedside two days before and hearing the knock. But he'd felt too dejected to answer the door, unable to face the well-meaning kindness of a neighbor.

"Well, so I'm here again to tell you," Mr. Rood was saying, "that if you want me to help unearth your Uncle Asa and show you what needs to be done, I'm willing."

Lucas stood dumbly, staring at his neighbor. Mr. Rood was being kind. He was offering to help Lucas perform a cure, a cure that would save Mama. But it was too late.

"It's no use!" Lucas cried. "Mama's dead."

11

"Dead?" It was Mr. Rood's turn to look stunned. "When—?"

"This morning," whispered Lucas.

"Oh, Lord," said Mr. Rood sadly. "Here I am, prattling on about Enoch's cure, and you still raw with your grief."

There was an awkward silence. "I'm sorry, son," said Mr. Rood. "If I'd known . . . well, I'd not have mentioned a word of it."

He reached out to touch Lucas's shoulder. "Your mama was real bad sick," he said. "It was most likely too late to save her, even if you had known what to do."

Lucas knew he should say something, but his mind was a whirl of confusion and pain as it slowly absorbed the full meaning of Mr. Rood's visit. Just two days before, when Mama was still alive, there had been a way to cure her!

"You come on home with me now, Lucas," Mr. Rood said. "Mrs. Rood will welcome any son of Hannah's as her own, and you and Enoch have always been companionable."

A terrible storm was gathering in Lucas's belly and rising through his chest. Mr. Rood's kind face, creased with concern, seemed to float before him. His insides were churning, and he felt sick with regret.

"Come, son," urged Mr. Rood gently. "We'll return tomorrow to take care of affairs here. Things will look better in the morning."

"No," said Lucas in a choked voice.

"Come now, Lucas," said Mr. Rood. "You can't stay here by yourself."

"Yes," said Lucas. "I—" He wanted to be alone, to sort out his chaotic thoughts. Why didn't Mr. Rood go away?

With effort, Lucas gathered his wits to reassure Mr. Rood and send him on his way. "I'll be fine, sir. Really. I thank you for coming and for trying to help. But there's things I need to do."

"All that can wait—"

"Thank you, sir, kindly. But I'll stay. For now."

Mr. Rood made several more attempts to talk Lucas into leaving with him, but Lucas remained firm. Finally, with a worried frown, Mr. Rood stepped to the door, saying, "I'll be back in the morning, Lucas, bright and early, and we'll see what's what. You try and get some sleep now."

Lucas sat at the table in the darkening room, thinking about the startling news Mr. Rood had brought. Enoch was alive, cured of consumption! The cause of the awful disease, which killed with agonizing slowness, was a mystery no longer. The dead returned to steadily drain life from the living. Yes, thought Lucas. That was just how it had seemed.

He knew he'd never be able to forget the way Lizy, Pa, Asa, and Mama had all weakened gradually, growing thinner and paler, and how nothing he did could stop it. He remembered Asa, with his easygoing ways, his good-natured grin made crooked by missing teeth. What dark urge would make Asa return to harm the people he loved? It was a mystery from the other side of the grave, beyond Lucas's understanding.

But, strange as Mr. Rood's story had seemed at first, Lucas did not doubt that it was true. Wasn't Enoch alive and well? And the others in—where was it?— Rhode Island?

How he wished he could turn back the clock just two days! He imagined himself answering the door and listening joyfully to Mr. Rood's news of a cure. He pictured the two of them digging up Asa's grave and—he didn't want to think about the rest. He didn't want to imagine the "signs" showing that Asa still "lived" after death. He hadn't asked how the "mischievous" dead were "put to rest."

It didn't matter now, anyway, he thought wearily. If only he'd made himself answer Mr. Rood's knock, Mama would be alive, as Enoch was. But whatever it was that the Roods had done to save Enoch, it was too late for Mama. He had failed her, he thought miserably.

Against his will, Lucas's mind filled with the image of Asa rising from his wooden coffin and returning to draw life from the living . . . Now only Lucas was left. In horror, he looked around the barren room, once filled with the sounds and smells of life. He saw only ghosts and shadows—and worse, the specter of Uncle Asa.

14

For a long while, Lucas sat in the cold, unlit house, considering remaining where he was and letting Asa come for him, to put an end to the sadness that seemed to be all that remained in his life. What right had he, after all, to be alive when everyone else in his family was gone? When, because of him, Mama was dead, too? If he'd answered Mr. Rood's first knock . . . If he'd learned of the cure then . . . If he hadn't been so tired and scared and ignorant!

He felt that he, too, deserved to die, but, with disgust, he realized that he didn't have the courage for that. To stay where Asa still lingered between the world and the grave, to be visited by Asa, to suffer the same slow painful death as the others and to suffer it alone—*no!* Nor could he bear to accept the pity and kindness of the Roods, to be the poor orphan boy living on the charity of others. He had to get away.

And so, wanting only to leave that place of sickness and sorrow, he struck off into the chill of the wintry night, not knowing where he was going, or caring.

Three

For two days Lucas wandered about the countryside, creeping into barns to sleep at night, finding heat and comfort from the warm bodies and breath of cows and horses and oxen. At last, dazed and dizzy with hunger, he came to a town. As he walked down the main street, his attention was caught by a sign posted outside a large house. The words wavered before his eyes as he read: HELP WANTED—INQUIRE WITHIN. Tentatively, he reached up to tap on the door.

A woman as tall and skinny as a sapling answered his knock. She stood before Lucas holding a rolling pin, her hands and the front of her apron dusted with flour. Peering at him with narrowed eyes, she said, "Well?"

"I—" His voice sounded hoarse and strange to his ears. He cleared his throat and tried again. "I saw your sign," he said.

"It's no sign of mine," the woman replied brusquely.

Confused, Lucas looked back at the sign. Maybe he'd imagined it. He turned to go.

"Wait!" the woman commanded. She stood at the door, looking him over. Finally, with a snort of disdain, she disappeared into the house, saying, "Stay there."

Lucas waited, leaning against the wall. His eyes began to close, and he didn't try to stop them. The icy wind blew down his neck, but he hardly cared. Maybe, he thought, he would fall asleep right there on the doorstep and never wake up . . .

He was startled by a gruff but kindly voice. "So you can read. That's good."

"Beg your pardon, sir?"

Piercing blue eyes gazed at him from the middle of a face and head covered with tangled white hair. "Don't disappoint me, now," the man said. "You did read the sign, didn't you?"

"Yes," Lucas replied.

The man nodded. "Good. Got to be able to read and write," he said, adding suddenly, "You can write, too, can't you?"

"Yes."

"Had some schooling, have you?"

"Some," answered Lucas. "When there wasn't work to be done."

"Name?"

"Lucas Whitaker."

"Age?"

"Twelve." The questions were coming so fast Lucas barely had time to think.

"Parents?"

Lucas opened his mouth, but nothing came out.

"Parents?" the man asked, more gently. "Family?"

Lucas swallowed. "Gone," he whispered.

"Speak up, lad. These old ears aren't what they used to be."

"They're dead."

The man stared at Lucas with a question in his eyes, but Lucas didn't say any more. His mouth was dry as dust.

"You look all done in, lad," the man commented.

Lucas didn't answer. What did he care how he looked?

"Been traveling awhile, I'd guess," the man observed, watching Lucas and stroking his beard.

"Awhile."

"Where from?"

Home, Lucas wanted to say. But it wasn't home any longer. "North of here," he said instead.

The man nodded, looking curiously at Lucas from under his bushy eyebrows. "You look strong," he said. "Do you have experience with hard work?"

Lucas drew a sharp breath as a picture of the rocky hillside behind the farm filled his mind. He saw himself struggling to dig in the stony earth, blinded by tears of sorrow and anger and fear. He forced the memory away.

"I have experience, all right," he answered bitterly.

"So, you can read and write and you know what work is. That's good. Are you a fair hand with horses?"

Lucas nodded. Since the time he'd turned seven, it had been his job to care for Barnabas, the horse, as well as the pair of oxen, Reuben and Rachel. The cow, Ruth, had been Mama's responsibility, along with milking, churning, and making cheese. Lizy'd helped with the chickens.

The man's question made Lucas's chest lurch with longing for the familiar velvety feel of Barnabas's nose, and for Reuben's and Rachel's patient, brown-eyed gaze.

Forget them, he told himself fiercely. They were Enoch Rood's to care for now. That part of his life was gone.

"Are you squeamish?"

The question interrupted Lucas's thoughts. Again he said, "Beg your pardon, sir?"

"Are you the type that's likely to go all swimmy-headed and jelly-kneed at the sight of a bit of blood?"

Lucas had helped with the butchering plenty of times. It wasn't his favorite chore, but he'd taught himself to get used to it. He thought of his mother's coughing, and of the bright red blood on her pillow that she had tried to hide from him. "I don't guess I am," he said.

"All right, then, here's my last question. Are you fearful of the dead, lad?"

19

Lucas looked up quickly, surprised. He wondered why the man was asking.

Was Lucas fearful of the dead? Afraid of his own dear mama, his strong, quiet pa, his sweet sister Lizy, the babies? He shook his head. Afraid of Uncle Asa, coming up from his grave to find Lucas and drain away his life, too?

"No!" he said, too loud.

With a lift of his eyebrows the man said, "Then I expect you'll do."

"Do for what, sir?" Lucas asked.

"Why, to work," the man answered, with a trace of impatience. "Isn't that why you stopped?"

"Yes, but—well, the sign didn't say what kind of help it is you're looking for."

"I am Uriah M. Beecher: doctor, dentist, apothecary, barber, and, when all else fails, undertaker. Call me Doc. Everyone else does. And you, lad, are my new apprentice."

Four

⁂

Uriah Beecher led Lucas into the house, talking as he walked. "The boy before you didn't last long. Hadn't the stomach for surgery. Wasn't much good around sick folks, said dead ones gave him the creeping willies. Which is why I asked your feelings about the subject."

Lucas didn't say anything more.

They entered the kitchen, where the tall, thin woman who had first answered the door was bending over to remove a pie from a large, iron cookstove. "The last boy worked too little and ate too much, in my view," she said tartly, straightening up and eyeing Lucas disapprovingly.

"I believe you have already made the acquaintance of my sister, Mrs. Bunce," Doc Beecher went on, ignoring her comment. "Cora, this is—pardon me, but what did you say your name is, lad?"

"Lucas Whitaker."

"Lucas Whitaker, who, by the looks of him, could use some good hot food and a sound night's sleep. Young man," he said, turning to Lucas, "I have some affairs to attend to, so I shall leave you in Mrs. Bunce's capable hands. I'd like for you to begin your apprenticeship tomorrow morning, if you're up to it."

After a sharp glance from his sister, he added quickly, "As soon as you've finished chores for Mrs. Bunce, that is. For your wages, you'll get Mrs. Bunce's fine cooking, a roof over your head, and a bed to sleep in."

Cora Bunce sniffed. "Not to mention learning the practice of a useful trade," she added.

"Ah, yes," said Doc Beecher with a laugh. "Of course. You shall benefit from the vast store of my knowledge, as well."

"If your work is satisfactory," Mrs. Bunce interjected.

"Yes, of course, Cora," Doc Beecher said soothingly. Lucas thought he saw the doctor look over at him with a sly wink, but it happened so fast he wasn't sure.

Doc Beecher put his hand on Lucas's shoulder. "You get some sleep now, lad," he said gently as he turned to leave.

At Doc Beecher's simple kindness, Lucas felt his throat close up, and he blinked back the tears that had suddenly sprung to his eyes.

Mrs. Bunce was eyeing him appraisingly. "You're filthy," she announced. "There's a washtub out the back door. Get yourself cleaned up."

Lucas went outside. He pumped some water into the washbasin, splashed his face, rinsed his hands, and, not seeing a cloth, wiped the dirt from his hands onto the leg of his trousers. When he turned to go back inside, Mrs. Bunce was standing in the doorway, her hands on her hips. "What do you think you're doing, young man?"

"I—I was just washing up, ma'am," said Lucas. "You said—"

She sighed and shook her head. "Bring that basin inside," she said impatiently.

Bewildered, Lucas did as he was told. Mrs. Bunce pointed to the stove, where a kettle of hot water steamed. "Use that," she said. "And this," she added, handing Lucas a cake of soap. "Leave your clothes outside. When you've finished, put those on." She nodded in the direction of a pile of clothes sitting on the table. "The last boy left them. I expect they'll fit suitably. Rub this through your hair," she continued, handing him a bottle and muttering under her breath. Lucas caught the words, "Probably crawling with vermin."

"Wash thoroughly now." She turned to leave, then stopped and added meaningfully, "Everywhere."

Lucas felt himself flush with a mixture of embarrassment and astonishment. The woman wanted him to take off all his clothes, wash his entire body with soap and warm water, and dress back up in someone else's —the last boy's—clothes!

But it was only the beginning of March, he wanted

to protest, and as cold and raw an evening as was possible to imagine. At home, they'd never have bathed on such a night. Mama always said it was best to wait until the wintry weather was over. The body built up its own protection from sickness and the like, she said, and no good came of washing it off. She used to sew Lucas's father into his long johns in the fall, and cut him out of them in the spring, to keep him safe from the cold.

A small voice inside reminded Lucas: But it *hadn't* kept Pa safe, not from consumption.

Feeling angry and uneasy, Lucas took off his clothes and set them outside the door. He looked over his shoulder to make sure Cora Bunce wasn't coming back into the room, then mixed the hot water from the kettle with the cold water in the washtub and, using the soap and cloth he'd been given, began to wash himself.

The soap was soft and slippery, not coarse like the soap his mama had made at home from lye and lard. It smelled sweet, like flowers, Lucas noticed, grimacing with distaste.

Blushing although no one was there to see, he washed everywhere and poured some of the strong-smelling liquid from the bottle onto his head, as the woman had instructed, rubbing it into his dark brown hair. He dried with a soft cloth and pulled on the last boy's shirt and trousers. Lucas was tall for his age, and thin. The pants were short and too big around the middle, but they were warm and, after he adjusted the suspenders, wearable.

He was dumping the wash water out the kitchen door when Mrs. Bunce came back into the room. Pursing her lips in disapproval, she said, "We don't dump waste all about the house. There's a place out behind the barn for pouring dirty water. And other filth."

"Yes, ma'am," said Lucas. Everything here was strange and different, and he felt too tired to take it in.

He closed his eyes. The aroma of the freshly baked pie sitting on the tabletop made him imagine for a moment that he was back home, with his mama humming cheerfully as she did her cooking over the big open hearth. But when he opened his eyes, instead of his mother's round, red cheeks and merry eyes, it was Mrs. Bunce's pinched nose and tight lips that greeted him over a bowl of porridge.

"Here," she said. "Eat that, then go to your room. It's the one off the parlor there. Chores begin at sunup."

Lucas tore his gaze from the pie and began eating the porridge. It was hot, at least, and filling, and he was glad to get it. He was hungry enough to eat twice as much, but remembering Mrs. Bunce's remark about the last boy and his unfortunate appetite, Lucas got up when he finished.

Without a word, the woman took the bowl away, and Lucas went down the hall in the direction in which she had pointed. He felt confused by all the rooms in this house. Was he to have one all to himself, he wondered. He and Lizy used to sleep together, within sight and hearing of Uncle Asa, Mama, and Pa. He didn't like the idea of sleeping alone.

The small room was sparsely furnished and spotlessly clean. There was a nightstand with a candlestick on top and a bed. The mattress was made of feathers, he noticed, instead of straw, and was covered with a quilt.

The pattern of the quilt reminded Lucas again of his mama, and for a moment he imagined her sitting by the hearth on a winter's evening, her eyes squinting against the darkness, her hands flying up and down and back and forth as she took pieces from her scrap bag and joined them into squares.

With a pang, he thought of the bed that he and Lizy had shared, and of the warm patchwork coverlet Mama had made. He wished that he'd brought it with him, but he'd left quickly, taking nothing.

Tired as he was, he lay on the bed in the darkness for a long time, his eyes open, thinking and remembering. Each night since he had buried his mother and left home, the same puzzling thoughts kept tumbling through his mind, keeping him from sleep.

Why, he wondered, did good people like Mama and Pa and Lizy and the babies—and, yes, Asa, too—have to die? For what reason, when everyone else in his family was gone, had his miserable life been spared?

Perhaps worst of all was the knowledge that he could have stopped the deaths, as the Roods had done. There was a cure for the ravages of consumption. Why, he asked himself, pounding his fist on the feather mattress, had he not learned of it before it was too late?

Five

❦

Lucas moved through the early-morning hours of his new life as if in a dream. Without thought or question, he obeyed Mrs. Bunce's orders to fetch water, chop and carry firewood, empty the chamber pots, and feed the chickens and horses.

A distant part of his mind noticed things about Doc Beecher's house that once would have interested him: thick carpets that covered the floors, stuffed furniture that was soft to sit on, mirrors and paintings on the walls, glass windows in a few of the many rooms, and a tall, wooden clock that startled him from time to time with its chiming. But he paid scant attention to any of it.

Once, he stopped short on catching sight of himself in the parlor mirror. They hadn't had a looking glass at home, and it was a moment before he recognized that the grim face looking back at him, with its dark brooding eyes, narrow mouth, and skin stretched tight over sharp, high cheekbones, was his own.

After a meager meal of bread and jam, he was sent to the front room, where Uriah Beecher sat reading by the window.

" 'Morning, lad," said the doctor, looking up from his book. "Have a good feed, did you?"

Lucas shrugged.

"Mrs. Bunce has a peculiar tendency to hoard the household supplies," Doc Beecher said with a little smile. "I expect she got that way from living with Horace Bunce, her late departed husband. He was the most miserly skinflint I've ever— But never mind that. However, I do have to watch that sister of mine, or she'd have me on bread and water. Which from the looks of her is all she ever eats."

When Lucas didn't respond, Doc Beecher looked at him over the tops of his thin gold-rimmed glasses. "Hmmm," said Doc. "Not much of a one for conversation, are you? Well, I suppose it's no wonder, all things considered. People talk when they're ready, I've found. All right, then. Let me put you to work."

Doc Beecher stood up. "You'll find out soon enough what it's like around here. One day nothing much happens, and the next all tarnation breaks loose.

"So I've learned to take advantage of the quiet times.

That's when I write in my journals, and work on my experiments and hypotheses. It's when you can make yourself useful sharpening my instruments, making up medicines, and generally helping me to be prepared for the next bout of human misfortune we'll need to deal with."

Lucas looked around the room. There was a long table covered with a sheet. Next to it were trays full of the doctor's medical instruments. Some Lucas recognized, such as a saw and several sizes and styles of knives, pliers, drills, and shears. Others were peculiar-looking, their uses unknown to him.

A pitcher and washbasin sat on a table near a large chair with leather straps attached to it. He'd never seen a chair like it and wondered what the straps were for.

All along the walls were shelves lined with a remarkable assortment of books, pamphlets, bottles with powders and liquids of different colors, and jars full of squirming leeches. There was a large drawing of a person without any skin on, so Lucas could see the bones and other inside parts, and on one of the shelves there was what appeared to be a human skull, with the teeth sticking right out of the jawbones.

Doc Beecher's desk held stacks of papers, a pen and inkstand, and what Lucas knew was an oil lamp, although at home they'd had only candles to light the darkness. There were two regular chairs, a fireplace, and the wood box Lucas had filled earlier that morning. Next to the door were saddlebags and a large black traveling bag.

"Today I'd like you to mix together equal parts of each of these ingredients," Doc Beecher said as he took several jars from the shelf, "and put the mixture in these little cloth pouches. Clear enough?"

"How much from each jar, sir?" Lucas asked.

"Call me Doc. As I said, everyone else does."

"How much of each . . . Doc?"

Doc Beecher handed Lucas a spoon. "Two spoons-ful."

Lucas began measuring and mixing. Doc Beecher went back to his papers. They were silent, which was fine with Lucas. He found the repetitious work oddly soothing. It demanded just enough of his attention that he didn't have to think about anything else, and the dried plants, whatever they were, smelled pleasant.

The morning passed quietly. Mrs. Bunce brought the midday meal: thick slices of warm bread, cheese, and wedges of pie. Lucas figured out quickly enough that Mrs. Bunce would feed him better when Doc was around to keep an eye on what she was serving, and he vowed to try to eat as many meals as he could in Doc's company.

After they ate, Doc Beecher gave Lucas some instruments and told him to put an edge on them. Lucas was just beginning to get a feel for honing the blades with the sharpening stone when there was a rapping at the door.

Doc stood and admitted a grinning young man who announced jubilantly, "I've come for barbering, Doc, the most important shave and haircut of my life. My whole future, you might say, rests in your skill at razoring."

"My, my," said Doc. "This sounds serious. Let me guess . . . Is someone going courting, perchance?"

A flush of pleasure colored the man's face. "Right you are, Doc."

"And, I wonder, would the lady in question be none other than Martha Pitcher?"

"Right again," said the beaming young man. "I've been calling on her all this winter long. Tonight, we're taking a sleigh ride and—"

"And you'll be asking her to marry you, out under the stars and the big white moon, is that it?" said Doc with a smile. "I hadn't marked you for quite such a romantic, lad. Well, well. That's fine."

Then, shaking his head, Doc pretended to be very serious. "I've got a formidable job ahead of me, though, if I'm to make the likes of you presentable. Moonlight or no moonlight, it's a good bit of help you're needing."

"Just get on with it, Doc," said the young man, laughing. "But I warn you, don't get carried away with the scissors." He wiggled his eyebrows up and down and whispered, "Martha has expressed a certain fondness for the way the hair curls round my ears."

Lucas continued working throughout this exchange, but he could feel his lips twitching into a smile. The young man's high spirits were hard to resist.

"May I present Lucas Whitaker, my new apprentice," said Doc. "Lucas, this young firebrand is James Freeman. Not much longer to be a free man. Or so he hopes," he added, then roared with laughter, greatly pleased with his joke.

James Freeman settled himself in the large chair with the leather straps, which, Lucas noticed, hung unused. Doc explained to Lucas how to place a steaming-hot cloth on the face to soften the whiskers, and how to mix up a lather for shaving. Then, while James sat with the hot cloth covering the lower half of his face, Doc began the haircut, still teaching his technique to Lucas as he worked.

"The most important thing is to cover up the victim's mouth as soon as possible," he said with a wink at Lucas. "That way, he can't talk back, you see."

Muffled protests came from under the cloth, and again Doc laughed heartily.

Lucas felt shy about joining in the good-natured banter, but it was fun to listen and to laugh. He hadn't heard much talk about happy things such as courting and marrying for a long time.

Even Mrs. Bunce's scowling face, appearing at the door to "find out what all the ruckus was about," did nothing to dampen the lighthearted mood in the room.

James told them his plans. He hoped to be married

in April, so he and Martha could set up housekeeping and be ready for the spring planting season.

When James Freeman left, his pink cheeks smooth and his hair glistening, Doc turned to Lucas and said approvingly, "That was a fine, sharp edge you had on the razor, lad."

Lucas, who was wiping the razor clean, ducked his head, pleased by Doc Beecher's praise.

Mrs. Bunce returned at that moment to ask, "Did you charge Mr. Freeman a fair wage for that shave and haircut, Uriah?"

Doc Beecher looked uncomfortable. "The man's mind was on wooing, not wages," he said.

"That's no excuse," Mrs. Bunce replied. "Do you want everyone in town marching in here for their shaves and haircuts, free of charge?"

"That's hardly likely," Doc Beecher murmured.

"Uriah," she said, a warning tone in her voice, "we can't expect to keep this household going on the earnings from my spinning. My fingers are nearly worn out. I've told you—"

"You have indeed, Cora," Doc said with a sigh. "I'll take care of it." To Lucas he said, "Lad, come here and I'll show you a little about the business end of our work."

Mrs. Bunce retreated as Doc Beecher took a large ledger book from the shelf and opened it.

"Have you a head for figures, Lucas?" he asked.

34

"I don't guess so," Lucas answered. "We mostly bartered with folks."

"That's generally the way it works here, too," said Doc. "Here are my accounts, such as they are. Now, take our young visitor, James, for example. Let me see . . ."

Doc ran his finger down several pages until he came to the entry for the Freeman family. "Here it is."

Lucas looked where Doc was pointing. From the series of notations, he was able to see that over the past few years, in return for such services as setting a broken finger, sewing up a leg wound, providing tonics for relief of ague and catarrh and plasters for bee stings, measles, and snake bite, Doc had received a variety of products from the Freeman farm, including eggs, milk, pork, and potatoes.

"After her husband died, Mrs. Bunce came here to Southwick from the city of Philadelphia. She's always urging me to be more businesslike, to set fees to be paid in cash and so on, the way they did in the city. But you know, lad, there's scarce little money to be found in a farming community such as this."

In Lucas's mind arose a memory of the small cloth bag his mother had kept under the straw mattress of her bed. Inside were four gold coins that Lucas had understood were to be spent only in the direst need. He'd left them behind, too, in his hurry to escape.

"You mark my words," Doc continued. "As soon as

he can, young James will be back with fair payment for our work today. Along with some tidings of a wedding, I'll wager."

"Yes, Doc," Lucas agreed.

"All in all, I find this system quite satisfactory. Now, you see here—"

Doc was about to point out a further aspect of his bookkeeping system when they were interrupted by another knock.

This time it was a woman, holding the hand of a boy several years younger than Lucas. The boy had a cloth wrapped round his chin and tied at the top of his head. Tears slid down his cheeks.

Lucas's Uncle Asa had had constant toothaches, and Lucas was pretty sure he recognized the look of misery on the young boy's face.

"Greetings, Dr. Beecher," said the woman. "Daniel here's got a tooth needs pullin', if you got the time."

"Good day to you, Mrs. Oaks," answered Doc. To Daniel he said, "Young man, what seems to be the trouble?"

The boy looked silently up at Doc, his eyes large and frightened-looking.

"I guess I can see for myself, can't I?" said Doc. "That face of yours looks swollen. Hurts bad, does it, lad?"

Daniel nodded and a little sob escaped his throat.

"All right, now. Daniel, this is my apprentice, Lucas. He'll help you into that chair."

Lucas took the boy's hand and led him over to the big chair where James had had his haircut.

"Can you climb up there yourself?" Lucas asked.

Daniel hoisted himself onto the high seat and looked fearfully at Lucas. Lucas looked to Doc, waiting to find out what he was to do next.

"Now, Daniel," Doc was saying as he assembled the instruments he would need, "Lucas is going to take those straps there and harness you up. It won't be for long. But I'm not going to lie to you, lad. This isn't going to be pleasant. I need you to be brave, and to stay as still as you can."

Daniel was looking at Lucas, terrified, while Lucas fastened the leather straps over his chest. Lucas tried to think of something, anything, to make the boy less afraid.

"You know why Doc Beecher uses these straps, Daniel?"

Daniel shook his head, his eyes growing even wider.

Lucas leaned down and began to whisper in the boy's ear. "Well, one day there was a man sitting there in that very chair. He had a bad tooth, see, same as you, and Doc was pulling it out. It hurt some, and the man got real mad at Doc and punched him right in the nose!

"I reckon Doc's afraid you'll do the same thing, so he's got to strap you down for his own protection, you being such a big, strong boy and him being so old and all."

Lucas stopped whispering when he saw that Doc stood ready to begin. Daniel glanced sideways at Doc Beecher, a flicker of a grin crossing his face.

"All set now, are we?" asked Doc.

Lucas looked into Daniel's eyes and lifted his eyebrows in a question. The boy nodded.

Doc untied the cloth from around the boy's head and said in a soothing voice, "Open wide. That's good. Now even wider. That's it, lad." With a small knife, he began to cut the pink skin around the inflamed tooth. Lucas felt Daniel's hand fumbling for his. Daniel's small fingers gripped Lucas's fiercely, and tears streamed down his pale freckled cheeks. Lucas's heart wrenched with pity.

Doc nodded his approval as Lucas, without being told, held the cloth where it would catch the flow of blood. With fascination, Lucas realized that the tooth was longer than it looked. Part of it was buried in the flesh, the way the roots of a plant were buried in the ground.

Once the length of tooth was exposed, Doc handed Lucas the knife and reached for a pair of pliers. The pliers looked fearsome. Daniel's eyes were squeezed tight.

Good, thought Lucas. It was better if he didn't see what was coming.

Doc grasped Daniel's tooth with the pliers and wiggled it back and forth with a steady pull. Daniel's body grew rigid and his fingers squeezed Lucas's so tight that

Lucas was afraid they might break. Slowly, the tooth emerged. Doc pressed a small piece of cloth into the hole in Daniel's gum, and held the tooth up for Daniel to see.

"There's the culprit," he said triumphantly.

At the sight of the tooth, Daniel let out a wail and began to cry in earnest.

"It's all right, Daniel," Lucas said, removing the straps. "It's over now. Soon you'll feel lots better, won't he, Doc?"

"It'll ache a bit tonight, lad," Doc said. "But nothing like before. In a day or two, you'll be right as rain."

Taking Daniel by the hand, Mrs. Oaks said, "What can we do by way of paying you, Doc?"

"I'll send Lucas over one of these days with the wagon. It could use a new wheel, if Eben has the time."

"We'll be expecting you, then, Lucas," said Mrs. Oaks.

"Yes, ma'am," said Lucas.

Doc wrapped Daniel's tooth in a bit of paper and asked the boy, "You want this, lad? Some folks like to keep their parts, others don't."

Daniel, still snuffling, pointed to Lucas.

"Ah, you want Lucas to have it." With a flourish, Doc handed the tooth to Lucas. "Here you are, Lucas. A memento of your first tooth-pulling." He smiled.

Not knowing what else to say, Lucas murmured, "Thanks, Daniel."

Mrs. Oaks said, "Lucas, when you bring the wagon,

why don't you stop by the house for a visit with Daniel? He seems to have taken a liking to you."

"Yes, ma'am," said Lucas. "I will." He felt oddly pleased.

When he and Doc were alone once again, and Lucas was wiping the blood from the knife and pliers, he could feel Doc looking at him.

"That was a nice touch you showed with the Oaks boy," Doc said. "I've often felt that it's not so much what we do when it comes to doctoring, as the kindness we show in doing it. I dread the times when I have to cause pain to a youngster such as Daniel. But you made it go easier for him."

Lucas kept busy straightening up the instrument tray, but Doc's words had stirred a warm glow in that deep, cold place inside him. Feeling Doc's eyes still on him, he looked up. Curiously, Doc asked, "What magical words did you whisper to that boy?"

"Nothing much," Lucas mumbled.

"Come on now, lad," wheedled Doc. "I let you in on all the secrets of my trade and you won't tell me what you said to bring a smile to that boy's face? I ask you, is that fair?"

"I thought he might be afraid of being strapped down," Lucas answered quietly. "So I told him a story. It—it's what my mama always did when I was scared."

"Ah, good thinking," said Doc. "And the tale?"

"It was only something I made up," Lucas said quickly.

"I'd like to hear it," said Doc.

Reluctantly, Lucas repeated his story. His voice trailed off at the end as he looked sideways at Doc to see how he'd react.

To Lucas's relief, Doc Beecher let out a great bellow of laughter. "Oh, that's a good one, lad. And where, may I ask, did you come up with a yarn like that?"

Encouraged by Doc's laughter, Lucas explained. "Back home, my Uncle Asa used to go to Emery Smith—he was the blacksmith—to have his teeth out. One time Asa had a toothache read bad, and he was drinking whiskey. To kill the pain, you know."

Doc nodded.

"Well, I guess he'd drunk a whole lot," Lucas went on. "By the time he got to Emery's place, he hardly knew where he was. Asa didn't remember it so good afterward, but I guess when he saw Emery coming at him with those pliers, he began to thrash about and he knocked Emery darn near senseless.

"Asa felt real bad about it when he sobered up. And, of course, he still had the toothache, too. But Emery wouldn't have anything to do with Asa after that. Told him he'd have to find somebody else to see to his tooth-pulling."

Doc laughed some more and shook his head wonderingly at Lucas. "You don't say much, Lucas my boy,

41

but when you do talk, you're worth listening to." He added, smiling, "I'm quite pleased with our day's work and with your part in it, lad. Now, shall we go see what Mrs. Bunce has fixed for supper?"

Lucas nodded. During the excitement of the afternoon, he had forgotten his sadness and shame about Mama's death, and his confusion about Uncle Asa. He'd felt, for the first time since all the sickness began in his family, something close to happiness.

Six

❧❧❧

Lucas spent the following morning doing chores for Mrs. Bunce, and it wasn't until the afternoon that he was able to join Doc Beecher in his office.

"Lucas, pull that chair over here and have a look at this," Doc said. He was seated at his desk, examining a chart. "I've been keeping this record for the past— what?—sixteen years," he explained. "It's a record of illnesses I've been called to treat. Now, see here, the way I've arranged it according to date of occurrence. The interesting thing to me, lad, is right here. There seems to be a pattern to the—"

At the sound of a timid tapping at the door, Doc stood and admitted a girl about Lucas's age. She pushed back the hood of her heavy cloak, releasing black curls that sprang up all around her face. Her cheeks were red from the wind and cold, and her blue eyes were large and solemn.

"You're one of Lewis Stukeley's daughters, if I'm not mistaken," said Doc Beecher. "Sarah, is it?"

"No," said the girl breathlessly. "I'm Lydia, sir. It's Sarah I've come about. She's doing poorly, Doctor. Mama's been dosing her, but to no good effect, and we're afraid it'll be like it was with—the others." Her voice dropped and tears filled her eyes. Quickly, she wiped them away and reached under her cloak, drawing out a cloth-wrapped bundle. "I came to see if you could help. Mama sent this. It's butter and some cheese, made up fresh this morning."

"That was very kind of her," said Doc Beecher, taking the package. "It was consumption, wasn't it, lass, that took the others?"

Lydia nodded.

"I thought so," said Doc with a frown. "Now then, Lydia, you came on foot, did you?"

Lydia nodded. "Yes, sir."

"Why don't you sit by the fire and warm yourself. I'll get my things together and Lucas here can hitch up the wagon. We'll go out to your place, and I'll have a look at Sarah."

"Thank you, Doctor," said Lydia gratefully.

"Lucas, I know you've not done it before, but see what you can do about preparing the wagon. I imagine Jasper and Moses are so eager to get out of the barn that they'll just about harness themselves. I'll be there shortly, if you run into difficulty."

As Doc had predicted, the horses were anxious to go. They stamped their feet, tossed their heads, and whinnied impatiently when Lucas entered the barn.

"Easy, there, Moses," Lucas said quietly, slipping the bit into the big horse's mouth. "Yes, Jasper, you're going, too," he assured the other prancing animal, fitting the harness over its soft brown ears.

By the time Doc Beecher appeared with his doctoring bag in his hand and Lydia by his side, Lucas had the wagon ready.

"Good, good," said Doc approvingly as he checked the reins. He helped Lydia up onto the seat and settled in beside her to drive. Lucas stood by, hoping that Doc wanted him to go along, too.

"Climb up here next to Lydia, Lucas," said Doc Beecher, "and the two of you see if you can arrange that blanket to keep out some of this confounded wind."

The horses set off at a rapid clip, their hooves crunching through the snow in a noisy rhythm. Soon they left the town of Southwick behind and were riding through the countryside. From time to time the wagon passed near a house or a farm, and Doc and Lydia talked about the people they knew who lived there.

"Everett Peck's cleared some more land," Doc observed. "Looks to be building on another room."

"Mrs. Peck's sister and family have come to stay," Lydia informed him. "Mrs. Peck will be having the baby soon," she added shyly.

"That makes, what, five little ones?" asked Doc.

"No, six, sir," answered Lydia. "Same as in our family." She stopped, and Lucas saw that her lower lip trembled. "Well, before this winter, and all the sickness . . ."

Doc took one hand off the reins, clasped Lydia's mittened fingers, and murmured some word of reassurance that Lucas couldn't hear.

Later, they passed a small, crudely built cabin with a thin trickle of smoke rising from the chimney.

"I wonder if old Moll Garfield is making it through the winter all right," Doc said, peering intently at the little house. "I should stop to pay her a call."

"I didn't much like walking past there today," Lydia said with a shudder. Turning to Lucas, she said, "Moll's an old granny woman. Some people go to her when they're sick, for cures and spells and herbs." In a low voice she added, "But other folks say she's a witch."

Doc was chuckling. "Now, Lydia," he said, "Moll's got her own ways some folks find peculiar, but she's no witch. I come here for ingredients for some of my medicines. She knows more about plants and what to do with them than anyone I know."

Lydia looked uncertain. "I heard she's an Indian . . ."

"Halfways," said Doc. "Her mother was full-blood

Pequot, but her father, Orvis Garfield, was a white man. It was Moll's mother who taught her the old Pequot ways, root healing and so on."

Lucas asked, "Who else lives there?"

"No one," answered Doc. "Moll's too ornery to marry, I expect." He chuckled. "Like me." Then, turning serious, he added, "That's one reason folks say the things they do. It unsettles them to see a woman like Moll, keeping to herself and doing as she pleases. But Moll doesn't belong in town. She never really belonged anywhere, I suppose. A lot of white folks, I'm ashamed to say, hold her Indian ancestry against her, and there's hardly another descendant of the Pequots left around these parts . . . or in all of Connecticut, for that matter."

Lucas looked back over his shoulder at the little cabin, feeling curious about the woman who lived there. Lydia looked back, too, and whispered, "Perhaps Doc's right. But with all the sickness, I do fear sometimes that . . . my family *has* been witched."

Lucas was about to speak of the cure the Roods had performed for their son Enoch, but he stopped himself. Perhaps Doc was waiting to talk it over with Lydia's parents. Lucas, remembering how peculiar he'd felt when Mr. Rood had told him of the remedy, was interested to see how Doc would go about explaining it to the Stukeleys.

Doc was saying, "Lucas, lad, as part of your education, I believe I'll send you over to spend a day or two with Moll, so you can see how things were done before the advent of our so-called modern medicine. How would you like that?"

With a shrug Lucas answered, "Well, sure, Doc. If you say so."

Lydia looked at Lucas with big eyes and, making a face, shook her head. Lucas smiled at her, acting braver than he actually felt about visiting the old witch woman.

By the time the wagon reached the Stukeley farm, the wintry sky was growing dark and a few snowflakes were beginning to fall. Lucas tied up the horses, then followed Doc Beecher and Lydia inside.

In the corner, a girl lay on one of the beds, coughing. Lucas looked away. He had been eager to come along on this trip, but hadn't been prepared for the rush of memories that assailed him when he walked into the Stukeleys' home.

It was a scene very familiar to Lucas. Mr. and Mrs. Stukeley and a little boy Lucas guessed to be about three years old were gathered near the hearth. In the winter his family, too, had lived mostly in the central room, even bringing their beds in from the only other room in back. The fire had been their source of light and heat during the long, cold days and evenings.

A kettle of water sat by the table. Hanging over the side was a ladle, which everyone in the family drank from. Another heavy kettle hung over the blazing fire, and a piece of meat sputtered on a spit.

The girl was taken with another long coughing spell. The harsh sound of it, the pained way in which she clutched her chest, and the thinness of her wrist when she did so made Lucas wince. He looked at Lydia, and in her eyes he saw a reflection of the anguish he had felt during the long months of his family's sickness.

"I've tried everything I know, Doctor," Mrs. Stukeley was saying. "I left the cow to graze in the moonlight, and made butter from the milk. I fed it to Sarah and gave her the cow's dung to smoke. She's had willow bark for the fever. But she's getting worse. It's just like—the others." She stopped, her voice breaking.

From the bed, Sarah looked up at Doc Beecher. She whispered weakly, "Thomas . . . came again . . . Doctor . . . last night . . ."

"What's that?" asked Doc.

"Thomas . . ." Sarah closed her eyes and fought for breath.

Mr. Stukeley spoke, looking uncomfortably at the floor. "She's been complaining of—visitations, I guess you could say. From Thomas."

"Thomas is—was—your eldest son?" Doc inquired uncertainly.

"That's right," said Mr. Stukeley.

Speaking carefully, Doc asked, "He passed on when?"

"This November past."

"Yet Sarah says that Thomas came to her . . ." Doc's voice trailed away.

"Comes to her, yes," Mr. Stukeley said awkwardly. "That's what she says."

"The others, Martha and Timothy, who died after Thomas, they said the same thing," said Mrs. Stukeley in a low voice. "They said Thomas came . . . in the night . . . and sat with them . . ." She paused, then finished quietly, "And caused them pain." She looked anxiously at Doc Beecher. "What can it mean?"

Lucas's heart began to beat fast as he listened to Mrs. Stukeley's words. He looked at Lydia, whose face wore the same worried, fearful expression as her mother's. Mr. Stukeley was looking hard at Doc Beecher, waiting for an answer. Lucas held his breath, waiting to see how Doc would respond.

Doc Beecher closed his eyes and appeared to be in pain himself. Opening his eyes, he said tiredly, "I cannot say what it means, though I've heard others speak of such things."

"We've heard tell of it, too," said Mrs. Stukeley cautiously.

"What I'm asking is," said Mr. Stukeley, "could it be Thomas who's making the others sick?"

Lucas leaned forward. Would Doc tell them about the cure?

"Thomas is dead, Mr. Stukeley," Doc said. His voice was flat, but not unkind.

"But they've seen him!" said Mrs. Stukeley.

"And if it isn't him, what is it that's taking my children, one after the other?" cried Mr. Stukeley. "Tell us, for mercy's sake! It's why you were sent for."

Sarah's coughing was the only sound in the room, except for the echo of Mr. Stukeley's desperate cry.

Lucas waited, anxious to hear Doc's answer. The Stukeleys' story sounded very much like the one told by Mr. Rood. Thomas Stukeley, like Mercy Rood, still "lived" after death. He was coming to the others from out of the grave and making them sick. Was it possible that Doc Beecher didn't know how to stop Thomas, the way Mr. Rood had stopped Mercy?

Maybe it wasn't too late to save Sarah!

Doc Beecher sighed and shook his head. "I wish I could give you the answer to your question, Mr. Stukeley. I don't know what brings on consumption, although I have my theories."

"Theories," repeated Mr. Stukeley bitterly. "Will your theories keep my Sarah from harm?"

Mrs. Stukeley looked at her husband and pleaded, "Lewis, please . . ." Her voice trailed off.

Doc Beecher said simply, "I'll do what I can, Mr. Stukeley. Lucas, hand me my bag, will you?"

Lucas jumped and ran to get the bag, which was by the door. Lydia reached for it, too, and for a moment their hands touched. Then Lucas handed the bag to Doc Beecher, who was feeling Sarah's cheeks and listening to her breathing.

Mr. Stukeley stood back, watching. Doc Beecher

asked for hot water to make a plaster for Sarah's chest. With the rest of the water, he made what he called a decoction, using one of the cloth bags of herbs Lucas had filled the day before.

"Have her drink this twice a day," he told Mrs. Stukeley, "and use this other medicine to make a fresh plaster every morning." He handed her the materials from his bag. "I'll leave enough for two days. I'll be back after that to see how she fares."

"Are you not going to bleed her, nor purge her?" asked Mrs. Stukeley.

"I don't believe it's efficacious with consumption, Mrs. Stukeley. There's little to be done, I'm afraid, other than to ease her suffering with the teas and plasters." Doc Beecher looked around the room and, with forced cheerfulness, added, "I've seen many worse cases. She may recover, Lord willing. Some patients do." Then, almost to himself, he muttered, "There's folks who'll tell you they know the reason why. But I'm not one of them. I'm sorry."

Lucas wanted to shout out the story of Enoch Rood's miraculous recovery, but Doc was in charge, and his quiet seriousness made Lucas reluctant to interfere. In an agony of indecision he wondered: Should he tell the Stukeleys about the cure he'd heard of from Mr. Rood, while there was still a chance to save Sarah? Doc had said he'd seen worse cases than hers, he told himself. Maybe that meant there was time. He'd have to ask Doc when they were alone.

Mr. Stukeley spoke then. "Thank you for coming, Beecher," he said stiffly. "I believe we'll doctor Sarah ourselves from here on."

All eyes turned to Mr. Stukeley, including Doc Beecher's. The two men looked at each other for a long moment. Then Doc bent over and closed up his bag. "As you wish," he said with a sigh.

At the door, Doc turned to say, "I shall pray for her speedy recovery. Good night."

As Lucas followed the doctor into the frozen night, he heard Lydia's voice questioning, "Papa?"

And Mr. Stukeley's grim reply: "I heard about a cure. And, by God, I aim to try it."

Seven

〜◉�〜

The sky had cleared and a delicate white saucer of moon was rising. Jasper and Moses, eager now for a bucket of oats and the warmth of the barn, pulled the wagon swiftly through the night.

Lucas sat on the seat next to Doc, who was strangely quiet, showing none of what Lucas had already come to think of as his customary ebullience. There were many questions Lucas wanted to ask Doc about what had happened at the Stukeleys', but Doc's silence and the pensive expression on his face made Lucas hold his tongue.

"That cursed disease!" Doc's sudden, vehement cry rang out over the snow-crusted fields. Holding the reins with one hand, he shook a fist in the air. "Good Lord, when will we be led out of the darkness of our ignorance and *enlightened?*"

For a while, neither Lucas nor Doc spoke a word, and the steady clop-clopping of the horses' hooves was the only sound. Then Doc turned to Lucas and asked quietly, "Did you come to me because you aim to become a doctor yourself someday?"

"No," Lucas answered truthfully. "I—I had nowhere else to go."

"Fair enough," said Doc. "If I recall correctly, you said you came from north of here. Had a farm there, did you say?"

Lucas nodded. Then, realizing Doc couldn't see him in the darkness, he replied, "Yes."

"But you couldn't stay there . . ." Doc said.

"I couldn't—I didn't—" He struggled with the words in his head, trying to figure out how to explain to Doc how the house had felt. Not empty, exactly, but full . . . full of the absence of everything and everyone he loved.

"Couldn't stay on alone, manage a farm all by yourself, is that it?" Doc asked.

"Yes," Lucas said. "After—after Mama died, I—couldn't see my way to stay."

"What did she die from, lad?" Doc asked gently.

"Consumption," Lucas said. "Same as what Sarah Stukeley has got. Same as what took my pa, and Lizy, and Uncle Asa, and maybe the babies, too, I don't know for sure."

He was about to bring up the cure when Doc began

to talk. "Lucas, lad, I went to medical college, did you know that?"

"No," said Lucas.

"Oh, yes. I went to what many would call one of the finest institutions. We performed surgery. We did dissections. We learned to practice 'heroic' medicine. We were taught that the body's fluids must be kept in balance. Sickness results from an imbalance of those fluids, we were told. Bad blood makes people sick, so we learned to bleed 'em, to get out the bad blood. We learned to bleed and blister and purge and puke our patients."

Doc snorted derisively. "And when that didn't work, we were told to bleed, blister, purge, and puke 'em some more.

"And you want to know something, lad? Any one of us who's got an honest bone in his body will admit that, half the time, we haven't the foggiest notion what we're doing. We don't know why our patients get sick, and we don't know why they get well, if they do. And when they do, I'll swear it's often in spite of us. There are days—and today happens to be one of them—when I think that if all our so-called medical knowledge were to be thrown in the ocean, it would be better for mankind." He added darkly, "And worse for the fishes."

Lucas didn't know what to say, but his silence didn't seem to matter to Doc. It was as if the day's events and the dark night had opened up Doc's heart and he seemed to want—to need—to talk.

"Many of my fellow physicians look down their noses at the 'quacks' who come around selling miracle cures and tonics from their wagons. They scorn the root doctors and granny women, like old Moll Garfield. Call them witches and worse."

They were at that moment passing by Moll Garfield's small cabin. Doc lifted his hat in a salute as they rode by. "But in truth, Lucas, their treatments are often as helpful as any doctor could give. You've heard of smallpox, of course," he said.

"Yes," answered Lucas. "Mama and Pa both lost family to it."

"A common experience," said Doc. "And now smallpox is hardly ever heard of, thanks to the discovery of inoculation. But when Dr. Edward Jenner first tried the vaccine back in 1796, he was laughed at by his fellow physicians. Think of it, Lucas! Who could credit the idea that giving someone a very mild dose of a disease would protect him from becoming deathly ill with it!

"Yet it's no different, on the face of it, from Moll Garfield's remedy for dog bite. She'll tell you to take a few hairs from the dog that bit you and apply them to the wound in a plaster. And I'll not tell you she's wrong. There's wisdom in some of the old ways. True, some are plain silly, and others are downright harmful. The trouble is, we don't always know the difference."

There was silence for several moments. Then Doc said in a low voice, "I was in Philadelphia in 1793 during the yellow-fever epidemic. Did you ever hear tell of it, lad?"

Lucas shook his head. "No."

"Oh, Lucas, the city was a ghastly place to be in that summer. Ghastly. People were nearly paralyzed with fear of the 'black vomit,' as they called it, myself included.

"I'll never forget the constant cry of the gravediggers ringing through the streets: 'Bring out your dead. Bring out your dead.'"

In the pale moonlight, Lucas could see Doc brush his hand across his forehead, as if to sweep away the memory.

"I was your age, lad, and thinking about studying medicine, when that fever swept through the city. Killed one out of every ten people, it did. Then it disappeared just as mysteriously as it had come.

"There wasn't a doctor in the city who could do more than hide behind closed doors, praying that he and his loved ones would be spared.

"That experience was a valuable lesson to me, Lucas. It has prevented me, I hope, from becoming arrogant. But it left me with the desire to *know more*. To be able to *do more*."

Doc Beecher turned to look at Lucas. Even in the dimness of moonlight reflected off snow, his eyes appeared to glow with the fervor of his words.

"I am humble before life's mysteries, Lucas. But I believe that we must try to learn and understand as much as we can, lad, if our being on this earth is to mean anything at all."

The town of Southwick lay ahead, quiet and still in the late-winter evening. Candle- or lamplight gleamed from a few windows; most were dark. As Doc steered the wagon down the empty main street, he turned to Lucas with a wry smile. "I'm sorry, lad, for bending your ear, and you a captive here in the wagon with no hope of escape. But visits such as ours to the Stukeleys today make me feel useless. Helpless. And that makes me melancholy.

"I expect you know something about that."

Tears sprang suddenly to Lucas's eyes. Useless. Helpless. Yes, he knew something about that. He was grateful for the darkness that hid his face.

Eight

ᴐᴑᏭᴑᴐ

The following morning Doc told Lucas to take the wagon over to Eben Oaks, the blacksmith, to have him look at the wheel.

"Tell him it was giving a bit of a wobble yesterday on the way out to the Stukeley place," Doc advised.

When Lucas stepped into the shop, young Daniel Oaks was counting out nails for his father, and placing them in bags to be sold. At the sight of Lucas, his face broke into a smile. "'Lo, Lucas," he said shyly.

"Hello yourself, Daniel," answered Lucas. "How's the toothache?"

"Gone," said Daniel, jumping up to give Lucas a look inside his mouth. The empty space looked much less red and swollen to Lucas. "Where's my tooth?"

"I gave it to an old man who didn't have any," said Lucas.

"Did not!" Daniel laughed.

"I did. Mighty grateful he was, too. He said to give you this." Lucas handed Daniel a twig several inches long. The end was splintered into bristles.

"What is it?" asked Daniel, wrinkling his nose in a frown.

"A tooth cleaner," said Lucas. "I made it for you. Doc says if you use it, it'll keep your teeth from going bad."

"Mama!" Daniel hollered excitedly, running out of the forge and into the house. "See what Lucas gave me!"

Lucas looked toward the man who had been busy heating a piece of metal in the forge. "Mr. Oaks?" he inquired.

"That's me," said the man. "I already know who you are. Heard all about you from Daniel and the missus. Just a minute, and I'll have a look at that wheel of yours."

Eben Oaks removed the red-hot piece of iron from the fire and, still holding it with his tongs, began to pound it on the anvil. Talking was impossible over the clanging of metal on metal, and Lucas was content to watch.

When Eben was satisfied with the shape, he dropped the horseshoe into a large tub of water to cool. There was a loud hiss when it hit the water.

Eben and Lucas walked out to the wagon. As Eben bent to examine the wheel, he said, "So, you're apprenticed to Doc Beecher."

"Right," said Lucas.

"You're lucky in that," said Oaks, running his hand around the wheel's rim. He flashed Lucas a knowing look. "Even if it puts you at the mercy of Cora Bunce."

Lucas shrugged. "She's not so bad, I guess."

Oaks was removing the wheel. "It's not a new wheel you're needing," he said. "I believe I can straighten this one up good as new."

He placed the metal wheel rim on the anvil and began turning it, tapping it lightly as he went along. Curiously, he asked, "Is she as persnickety as folks say? Mrs. Bunce, I mean. Mrs. Oaks heard Cora holds the notion that folks ought to wash themselves—all over, mind you—every so many days!"

"She's persnickety about that, all right," agreed Lucas.

"I say it's not natural," said Eben with a shake of his head. "I said to Mrs. Oaks, I said, it's like rubbing a fish in dirt to set a person in water like that. And this time of year!"

Lucas smiled. Pa would have said "Amen" to that. He decided to ask Doc's opinion about bathing the next time he had the chance. He was very anxious to talk to Doc about the cure for consumption, also, and vowed to himself to do that soon.

62

With a final stroke of his hammer, Eben removed the wheel from the anvil, held it out at arm's length, and with one eye closed examined his work. Evidently satisfied, he started for the door.

As he attached the wheel to the axle, Eben said, "I had a hard time of it when I was your age. Apprenticed to the devil himself, I was. Old Milton Yale. He's dead and gone, with no one to miss him, I can assure you of that. When he wasn't pounding on the anvil, he was pounding on me."

Lucas grimaced. He'd heard stories of masters who used their apprentices cruelly. He guessed Eben was right: it was luck that had brought him to Doc instead of to someone like Milton Yale.

"Now, you tell Doc that wheel ought to be good for a long while yet," Eben said. "And thank you for your kindness to Daniel. Mrs. Oaks said you had a right healing way about you."

As Lucas drove the wagon back to Doc's house, he repeated Eben Oaks's words to himself: "A right healing way about you." He liked the way they sounded.

Nine

೭ഄ൏ൟ൏ഄ

Lucas pulled the wagon up to the barn and was about
to unhitch Jasper and Moses when Mrs. Bunce called
from the doorway. "Leave the horses be, Lucas. Dr.
Beecher's needed at Clem Buell's place. He's been waiting for you."

She disappeared into the house, and Lucas guessed
she was going to tell Doc Beecher he'd returned. He
was curious, and eager to see what he and Doc would
be doing next.

Doc came out then, his black bag in one hand, a
wooden crutch in the other, and sat beside Lucas
in the wagon. "You drive," he said, and pointed the
way.

"I'm afraid of what condition we'll find Buell in, Lucas," he said. His face looked worried as he settled him-

self beneath the blanket. "He hurt the leg over two weeks ago and didn't send for me until now. His nephew Nat tells me it looks bad."

Lucas urged the horses forward. "The wheel's fixed, Doc," he said. "Mr. Oaks said you didn't need a new one. Said to tell you this one should last a while yet."

"Eben's a good man," Doc answered distractedly. "Honest as the day is long."

"Yes, Doc," said Lucas. He could see that Doc's thoughts were on Clem Buell, rather than on the wagon wheel. This was clearly not the time to discuss bathing or the cure or anything else with Doc. Keeping the horses at a lively trot, he waited until Doc pointed to a run-down shack on the edge of a large stretch of woods.

"That's Clem's place," Doc said.

Lucas stared. The house that he had shared with his family was small, dark, and rustic compared to Doc Beecher's house in town, but Clem Buell's place was far cruder. Made from ill-fitting boards with no chinking between them, the walls leaned haphazardly under a wearily sagging roof. The door hung open, and the single small window held neither glass nor oiled paper, but was stuffed with what looked like an old hat. The filthy snow was littered with broken dishes and tools, bones, food scraps, and the emptied contents of the household's chamber pots.

Doc Beecher appeared not to notice. He eased out

of the wagon seat, showed Lucas where to tie up the horses, and hurried into the shack. Lucas followed.

It took a moment for his eyes to adjust to the darkness inside. A large man lay on the floor on dirty blankets. Even in the dim light, Lucas could tell from the hollow planes of his face that all or most of his teeth were missing. His face showed several days' growth of whiskers. As Lucas looked closer, he could see the red flush of fever on the man's cheeks and the glazed look of his eyes.

Doc Beecher was kneeling at the man's side. "Clem?" he said loudly. "It's me, Doc Beecher. Can you hear me, Clem?"

Clem looked wildly about. "Lizbeth!" he cried. "Lizbeth! Lizbeth?" His voice faded and his eyes closed.

Doc leaned over to pull back the blanket. Lucas gasped when he saw the man's leg. It was swollen to at least twice its size, straining Clem's pants to near bursting.

A thin, nervous-looking man appeared in the doorway. Lucas guessed it was Clem's nephew when he said, "He didn't want no doctor is why I didn't come sooner. It was a tree fell on it. He was working alone, Doc. I didn't find him till the next day."

"I understand, Nat," said Doc. "You did right to come for me today. I'm going to have to take that leg off."

Nat looked sick. "He'll be awful riled about that, Doc. He'll—there's no telling what he'll do."

"He won't be saying or doing anything if I don't remove that leg," said Doc firmly. "You can see how rotten it is. A few more days and it'll kill him."

Nat turned away and slipped out the door.

"Leave that door open," Doc called after him. He muttered something about the air being thick enough to cut with a knife. To Lucas he said, "Looks like we're on our own. Get a good hot fire going, and look around and see if there's any whiskey."

As he built the fire, Lucas watched Doc remove from his bag a knife, a saw, a pair of tongs, a flat, metal plate with a handle on it, and a tin container. He handed the container to Lucas.

"Hang this tar near the fire to soften." He clamped the tongs onto the metal plate and directed Lucas to place it so that the plate was directly in the hottest part of the flames. "You find any whiskey?"

Lucas handed Doc the jug.

"Get as much of that down his throat as you can," Doc said. He began to cut away the leg of Clem's trousers.

It was difficult to get the delirious man to swallow the whiskey, but Lucas did his best. Doc reached over, took the jug, and gulped down a big swig for himself. Then he said, "Hold him, Lucas. Hold him hard. He's going to fight you, and I need you to keep him still. Keep giving him whiskey if he'll take it."

Doc worked quickly and skillfully and soon the amputation was over. Lucas knew he'd not soon forget the sound of Clem's strangled cries, or of the saw working through bone, or the strength of the man's struggle. Doc went to the fire, grasped the tongs, and touched the red-hot metal plate to the place where Clem's leg now ended above the knee. Clem, mercifully, fainted.

Lucas felt himself grow dizzy, and everything in the room began to look far away and fuzzy. Doc caught him as he fell and held him up, handing him the whiskey jug. Lucas took a deep swallow, and the terrible burning of the liquid brought him, choking and spitting, to his senses.

"There's no shame in feeling lightheaded the first time, Lucas," Doc said. "You're human, lad, not a chunk of stone." He continued to talk, quietly and matter-of-factly, instructing Lucas about the procedure he had performed.

"I had to cauterize the wound, you see, to stop the bleeding. Now I'll seal off the leg with this tar, see?— like that—and, Lord willing, the putrefaction will stop and Clem will get well."

Doc went to the door and called, "Nat? It's over. You can come in now."

Lucas listened while Doc explained to Nat how to care for Clem. "Keep giving him whiskey for the pain. And boil this in water and make him drink the water. It should help with the delirium. Those blankets he's lying on are filthy. If you haven't any clean ones, stop by and I'll have Mrs. Bunce give you some. I've left the crutch for when he's up to walking, but I'll be back to see how he's doing before that time comes, I should imagine. You tell him I'll fix him up with a wooden leg as soon as he's ready."

Nat had been staring fearfully at Clem the whole time Doc was talking. The man's agitation was so great that Lucas doubted he had heard a word Doc said. When Doc was finished, Nat kept repeating, "He's gon' be riled. He's gon' be awful riled, Doc."

"I'll be back, Nat, to talk to him," Doc assured the little man. "He'll be angry, no doubt about that. But it's his own confounded fault he let it go so long. The truth is, he's lucky to be alive, the stubborn old coot, and you can tell him I said so."

Ten

When Lucas reported for chores the following morning, Mrs. Bunce was not waiting impatiently in the kitchen to outline the duties she expected him to perform, as she usually was. He went to the barn to feed and water the horses and chickens. When he returned, she was standing at the cookstove.

"I've been with Uriah," she reported. "He's feeling a bit puny today."

She caught Lucas's worried look. "He says it's nothing to be concerned about. He's just worn out, I do believe. I've told him time and again, he's too old to be gallivanting around the countryside the way he does. You have an office, I tell him. Have your patients come to you, I say, the way they do in the city. But it's like talking to the fence post," she finished querulously.

"I don't guess Clem Buell could have made it here, Mrs. Bunce," Lucas murmured. "His leg was awful bad."

Mrs. Bunce looked at Lucas. "You may be right about that, young man. But I can't help worrying about Uriah. He lets people take advantage. If something were to happen to him, well, I—" Her face crumpled for a moment. She quickly adjusted her features to their customary stern appearance, but not before Lucas had glimpsed the fear in her eyes.

Why, Lucas realized with surprise, beneath her peevishness, she was really very fond of her brother. Somehow that made him feel more kindly toward her.

"He'd like you to pay a visit to the Stukeley family today," Mrs. Bunce went on. "After you've finished up your chores," she added.

"Are you sure?" asked Lucas uncertainly. "Mr. Stukeley said he wouldn't be needing Doc anymore."

"Yes, Uriah said that Mr. Stukeley had made that clear. However, he said he can't help wondering how the girl—what's her name?"

"Sarah," Lucas answered.

"How Sarah is faring. You know how he is. I tell him he's more concerned for his patients than they are for themselves." Shaking her head, Mrs. Bunce sighed. "In any event, he seems to think you could pay a visit without appearing to intrude. There's a girl about your age you could call on?"

"Lydia," Lucas supplied eagerly, feeling his neck

71

flush. He found that he did want to see Lydia Stukeley again, and he very much liked the idea of another trip through the countryside. The fact that Doc trusted him to make such a trip alone pleased him greatly. And while the sorrow that hung over the Stukeley household was a painful reminder of his own losses he, too, wanted to know if Sarah was any better.

"All right," said Lucas.

"You're to take Jasper," said Mrs. Bunce.

Lucas nodded happily. Jasper would be good company.

It seemed to Lucas that Mrs. Bunce was determined to get as much work out of him as she could, with Doc out of the way. By the time he finished up his chores, it was the middle of the afternoon.

The sky was flat and gray, threatening more snow, when Lucas finally headed out of town. Sitting astride Jasper, breathing deeply of the sharp winter air as it mingled with the steamy warmth rising from the horse's broad back, he wished more than ever that he had asked Doc about the cure and why he hadn't used it for Sarah.

He recalled overhearing Mr. Stukeley's grim voice saying, "I heard about a cure. And, by God, I aim to try it." If Sarah was no better, he decided he'd tell the Stukeleys what Oliver Rood had told him. He had a feeling it would be no surprise to Lewis Stukeley.

Following roughly the same route he'd ridden over

with Doc two days before, he arrived within sight of the Stukeley farm just before dusk. He tied Jasper and was about to knock on the door when he saw dark figures silhouetted on the hillside.

Squinting his eyes, he made out Mr. and Mrs. Stukeley, and the smaller figures of Lydia and her little brother, Samuel. Mr. Stukeley held a shovel in his hand. Lucas almost hollered a greeting, but something about the stillness of the huddled group stopped him. As he drew nearer, he saw that their heads were bowed in prayer. His heart gave a sickening lurch. Sarah! They were burying Sarah. Filled with dread, Lucas waited a distance apart.

When the family raised their heads, Lydia caught sight of him. "Here's Lucas," she said. A smile crossed her face. Then she quickly grew somber again.

Mr. Stukeley nodded. Mrs. Stukeley looked at her husband uneasily before she said quietly, "Good day, Lucas."

The family stood frozen, staring at him. There was no hole in the ground, no wooden box. Lucas had the strong sense that he had interrupted them, but not, thank goodness, in burying Sarah.

Under a small stand of hickory trees, Lucas could see flat fieldstones set upright in the ground. Without asking, he knew that they marked the graves of Lydia's brothers and sisters, along with others of the Stukeleys' relatives and ancestors.

"I—Doc wanted me—I mean, I wanted to know

how Sarah—if the plasters helped her any," he stammered.

"She's dying," Lewis Stukeley said. His voice was soft, but in it Lucas could hear anger and something else. Determination. "And we aim to do what we can for her."

"Yes, sir," said Lucas. Looking again at the shovel in Mr. Stukeley's hand, he was certain that he knew what they planned to do. "Would you like a hand, then, with the digging?" he said. The words were out of his mouth before he knew he meant to speak them.

Mrs. Stukeley drew in a sharp breath.

"It's no business of yours—" Mr. Stukeley began.

But Lucas interrupted him. "Where I came from, north of here, there's a man named Oliver Rood. His son Enoch was dying of consumption. Mr. Rood figured Enoch's sister Mercy was the one making Enoch sick. Mercy died first, you see, same as your Thomas. Mr. Rood said Mercy came back to—to 'make mischief,' he called it."

The Stukeleys were watching him closely, their faces guarded. He remembered how Mr. Rood had come to him in friendship, offering to help cure his mother. He was too late to save Mama, he thought fiercely, but at least he could be of use to the Stukeleys. It seemed, suddenly, terribly important that they allow him to help.

He plunged on. "Mr. Rood told me he unearthed Mercy's grave and put her to rest."

Lucas looked into Mr. Stukeley's eyes. "I don't know how he did it, exactly. But, after that, Enoch got well."

Mrs. Stukeley spoke carefully. "We heard something about that."

"Do you know what to do—afterward?" asked Lucas.

"Aye," said Mr. Stukeley. He seemed to make up his mind about something. "Lydia, run and get the other shovel for Lucas."

Lydia, Samuel, and Mrs. Stukeley stood by silently as Lucas and Mr. Stukeley together dug slowly into the earth. There was a thin layer of snow, and the ground was frozen down several inches, but the digging became much easier after that. At last, Lucas's shovel hit the wood of the coffin lid. Gently, they scooped the remaining dirt away.

Mr. Stukeley took a deep breath and lifted the lid. Inside lay the body, wrapped in a sheet of plain muslin fastened down the front with pins. Tenderly, Mr. Stukeley unpinned the cloth and opened it.

"Thomas!" cried Lydia. Her hand flew to her mouth. Her eyes looked enormous.

Mrs. Stukeley's head was bowed again in prayer, her lips moving silently. Little Samuel clutched her hand and buried his face in her skirt.

"He could almost be sleeping," Mr. Stukeley said wonderingly. "But see how his fingernails have grown . . . He does live!"

Lucas, too, stared at the body, transfixed. The boy looked to be the same age as Lucas. The flesh of his face was full, though bluish in color, and his eyes were fixed and open. Lucas had never seen Thomas Stukeley in life, but the young man in the coffin did look oddly vital. Lucas's mouth felt dry, and he could hear the blood pounding in his ears.

"He does live," murmured Mr. Stukeley. "He does live." He looked up at his wife and, for a long moment, their eyes remained locked. Mr. Stukeley looked away. "You know what I have to do, Anna," he said, almost in a whisper. "Take Samuel and Lydia—"

"Yes," said Mrs. Stukeley. She leaned down, picked up Samuel, and held him in one arm. With the other hand, she grasped Lydia by the wrist and began to walk down the hillside to the house.

Mr. Stukeley murmured another prayer, his voice so low that Lucas heard only the words, "God help me." Then he took a small knife from his pocket and, ever so gently, cut into Thomas's chest. Lucas's hand flew to his own breast as he watched.

"They said to find the heart," Mr. Stukeley said, in a voice so low he might have been talking to himself. "They said it would be here. Yes, that must be it . . ." Mr. Stukeley examined Thomas's heart. "Living blood," he said softly, "just as we were told."

Very carefully, he removed the heart, wrapped it in his handkerchief, and set it carefully on the snow-covered ground. Then he pinned the sheet closed over Thomas's body. Together, Lucas and Mr. Stukeley put the lid back on the coffin and covered it with dirt once more.

Mr. Stukeley carried Thomas's heart back to the house, where Mrs. Stukeley had the fire blazing. Lucas watched, transfixed, as Sarah was brought over to the hearth. Mr. Stukeley placed the heart in the flames. As it burned, Mrs. Stukeley fanned the smoke into the room, toward Sarah, who breathed deeply of it. Then the others, too, moved closer to breathe in the smoke. When the flames died down, Mrs. Stukeley gathered the ashes, mixed them with water, and gave the potion to Sarah to drink.

Lucas joined the family in a prayer for Sarah's recovery, then made ready to leave. The family was quiet and subdued, as befitted such a solemn ritual. But, afterward, there was something new in the room and in the faces of the Stukeley family. It was hope. Lucas could feel it filling his own heart as well, as he rode slowly back to Doc's in the darkness.

When he had rubbed down Jasper and given him an extra portion of oats, Lucas stopped by the next stall to give Moses's nose a rub. "Sorry for leaving you behind, Moses," he said. "But I couldn't very well ride the both of you, now, could I?"

Moses rolled his eye, but moved his head so Lucas could rub between his ears.

"Come on, boy." Lucas coaxed him with a laugh. He

continued to talk soothingly as he scratched the big horse's head. "Don't be feeling sorry for yourself. I'll take you next time, how's that?" With a final pat to Moses's smooth back, Lucas went to the house to find Doc Beecher. He couldn't wait to tell Doc what had happened at the Stukeley farm.

To his disappointment, he was greeted in the kitchen by Mrs. Bunce, who said, "Dr. Beecher has gone to bed, Lucas, and at this late hour I've already had my supper. I've kept yours warm. But, first, it's time for you to bathe."

At the mention of supper, Lucas's stomach growled, and he looked longingly at the pot that sat on the cookstove.

"There's hot water and soap and, as you can see, I've washed your clothes."

Lucas sighed. So it was to be another bath. He thought of Eben Oaks asking, "Is she as persnickety as they say?" and his lips twitched in a smile. Once again he promised himself that he'd ask whether Doc held to all this washing and bath-taking.

Doc. He'd been feeling "puny" that morning, and had gone to bed early. "How's Doc?" Lucas asked Mrs. Bunce. As soon as he asked the question, he realized he was afraid to hear the answer.

"Much better, he says," she answered briskly. "You be sure and wash up properly, mind you," she said, turning to leave the room.

"Yes, ma'am," said Lucas.

Shivering as he undressed, Lucas wished again that Doc was awake so that they could talk over Sarah Stukeley's cure. Washing himself "properly," as he'd been instructed, he marveled at how much his life had changed in the short time since he had come to be apprenticed to Doc Beecher. Here he was, he thought, grinning sheepishly, taking his second bath in only—what?—five days.

But it was more than just the bathing. More, too, than the big house with all the fine and fancy things in it, that made his life here so different. Lucas struggled to fix in his mind just exactly what it was that felt so new. It was something about Doc himself. It was the way Doc talked to Lucas.

At home on the farm, life had been hard. Mama, Pa, Asa, and Lucas himself had all worked from sunup to sundown just to finish the chores. When dark came, they usually fell into exhausted sleep. There was laughter and there was talk, sure, but most often it was about the crops or the weather, or the work that had to be done the next day.

Pa had been, for the most part, a quiet man. Mama was the one who told Lizy and Lucas stories and read to them from the Bible. But no one had ever before talked to Lucas the way Doc had talked in the wagon the night they'd left the Stukeleys together. Doc asked big questions about things that Lucas had wondered about but had never really thought to put into words. He felt as if Doc's talking had loosened up all those thoughts inside him, and now they wanted to come pouring out. Doc's talk put Lucas in mind of a world bigger than the farm, bigger than Southwick, a world that was thrilling and mysterious. It made him want to know more.

He'd felt helpless and ignorant, watching his family die. If only he'd known then what he knew now! Sometimes doctoring meant doing unpleasant things, such as pulling Daniel's tooth or taking off Clem Buell's leg. But now that those things had been done, Daniel was feeling better and Clem would live. Working with Doc had shown Lucas how good it felt to be able to help people who were sick or troubled.

And tonight, on the ride home from the Stukeley farmstead, he had felt exhilarated. Now that Thomas Stukeley had been unearthed, his heart burned, and the cure completed, Sarah Stukeley would live, too. Lucas was sure of it.

Eleven

Lucas was relieved to find that Doc Beecher was up and about the next day.

"Merely the aches and pains of old age, lad," he assured Lucas with a wink. "I dosed myself and ordered myself to bed for the day and now I feel quite well again, despite the old saying about doctoring oneself."

"What old saying is that?" asked Lucas.

"Why, lad, have you never heard it said that he who doctors himself has a fool for a physician?"

Lucas smiled and shook his head.

"Well, now you know me for what I am," Doc said, laughing. "But, be that as it may, this old fool feels full of spit and vinegar today. And how about yourself, lad? Tell me about your visit with the Stukeleys."

Lucas and Doc Beecher were sitting in Doc's office.

Eagerly, Lucas pulled his chair closer to Doc's and began to talk. "When I got there, Doc, I saw Lydia and Samuel and Mr. and Mrs. Stukeley all standing together on the hillside. They were praying, and looking real sorrowful."

Doc winced. Lucas, seeing the look on Doc's face, hurried on. "I thought at first they were burying Sarah, but they weren't. Remember, Doc, how they said that Thomas was visiting Sarah, and that he'd visited the others, too?"

Doc, a wary look on his usually jovial face, nodded.

"Well, it's just as Mr. Rood said to me the day—"

"Mr. Rood?" asked Doc.

"Oliver Rood. His farm neighbored ours. He came to me when—well, when he thought there was still time to save my mama. And he told me that he knew a cure for her. He'd used it, you see, to save his own son Enoch. And it worked, Doc!"

Doc Beecher lifted his eyebrows but said nothing, waiting for Lucas to continue.

"And now word of the cure is spreading, must be. The Stukeleys heard of it from some kinfolk. And so when I got to the farm and saw Mr. Stukeley with a shovel in his hand and no burying to do, I figured I knew what they were about. I wanted to help, and Mr. Stukeley said I could."

Lucas stopped to look at Doc. He realized he'd been expecting—hoping—that Doc would be pleased at this news. Mr. Stukeley had dismissed Doc, but he'd allowed

Lucas, Doc's apprentice, to be involved in performing Sarah's cure. Lucas had felt proud of that, and had thought Doc would be, too.

But Doc only asked quietly, "Help?"

"Yes. With the digging. See, Thomas was the first to die."

"And Thomas was coming round to make Sarah sick," Doc said.

"That's right," said Lucas. "So we dug up his grave and, Doc, when we opened up the coffin, Mr. Stukeley saw the signs that Thomas still lived."

"What signs were those, lad?" asked Doc.

"He looked—well, like himself, I guess. And there was living blood, Mr. Stukeley said, in his heart. His eyes were open and his fingernails, Doc! They had grown."

"And then?"

"Then Mr. Stukeley took Thomas's heart. And they burned it so Sarah and everyone could breathe the smoke, and then Mrs. Stukeley made a medicine from the ashes, and Sarah drank it, and it will make her well!" Lucas finished triumphantly.

"You say this Mr. Rood told you of the cure after your mother had passed away, Lucas?" Doc asked gently.

Lucas looked away. "He came to tell me before, but—"

"But what, lad?"

Lucas swallowed back the lump that had risen in his

throat at the thought of how close he had come to being able to save his mother. "But I didn't go to the door . . . not until two days later, when Mama was gone."

There was a silence. Then Doc asked, "Who was the first to die, lad?"

"Uncle Asa," said Lucas. "Mr. Rood figured it was Asa who was—the mischievous one."

Doc cleared his throat, looking disturbed.

"I didn't really understand the cure, how it worked. But now I do, thanks to you."

Doc appeared startled. "How's that, Lucas?"

Lucas was surprised by Doc's question. "Well, you said—you said—lots of things. You said doctors don't always know what to do."

Doc smiled bleakly. "True enough."

"And you said that old witch woman—"

"Moll Garfield?"

"Yes. You said she knows a lot even though people call her a witch, and if she used hair from a dog that bit you it might cure the bite. And you told me how you can protect yourself from getting smallpox real bad by making sure you get just a little bit of it. So, when I thought about the cure, the one Mr. Stukeley did . . ."

"Yes?"

"Well, it seemed the same." Lucas stopped. All the things he was trying to explain to Doc had fit together perfectly when he'd thought about them. But somehow saying them aloud made his thoughts sound foolish. He tried again.

"So it seemed to be the same kind of cure . . . to take some smoke from the fire and to make medicine from the ashes, ashes that came from the thing that was making Sarah sick . . . Like a—what did you call it? A noc—?"

"Inoculation," Doc said softly.

"It seemed like that. And, at first, when Mr. Stukeley began to cut into Thomas, I got a shivery feeling and I thought maybe we were doing wrong. But then I remembered you said that in medical college you did dissections, and isn't that—well, doesn't that mean cutting into bodies that are dead?"

"It does, indeed," answered Doc.

"So I figured it was all right. And you said you learned about bleeding people to get the bad blood out. And you had to cut off Clem's leg, because it was the bad part that was making the rest of him sick. So I thought taking the heart out—"

"I can see how you were thinking, lad," said Doc.

But that wasn't all. There was something else Lucas wanted to explain. "Remember you said that sometimes you think the good of what you do isn't in what you do so much as in the—the kindness you show in doing it?"

"You don't miss much, do you, lad?" asked Doc with a tired smile.

Lucas sat quietly for a moment, trying to find the

right words for the certainty that had been growing within him ever since his visit to the Stukeley farm. Finally, taking a deep breath, he began, "I *know* Sarah will get well. I can't say how I know. I—Mama's gone, but I could help the Stukeleys. It felt right, what we did."

It was coming out all mixed up. But it *was* all jumbled up together. That was what made it so hard to explain. He wished he could find the words for what he knew inside: that his mama's unnecessary death was the very thing that made him so sure that Sarah would live, that his grief and regret over his mama's dying meant he was the right person to bring about Sarah Stukeley's cure. Because he had not used it to save Mama, the cure *had power*. It was only right that he should be able to use it to help Sarah Stukeley. He felt this in his heart, but he didn't know how to make Doc feel it, too.

"Lad," said Doc, "it's true I said all those things. It's true that doctors, including myself, are far from knowing all the answers. But there are some things we do know, Lucas, and one is that when people are dead and buried, as Thomas was and as your Uncle Asa was, they cannot come back to do us harm.

"This belief your neighbor and Lewis Stukeley hold is based, not on scientific reasoning, lad, but on superstition, and fear, and ignorance. And while it is easy to understand why they would want to believe in it, for the sake of holding out hope that their loved ones will get well, it—"

"I was ignorant before," said Lucas, his voice rising. "Now I know! Sarah Stukeley *will live*."

"I hope you're right about that," Doc said with a sigh.

"But you don't believe it."

"She may live, but it won't be because of what was done to Thomas Stukeley's remains." Doc looked almost pleadingly at Lucas's face. "I believe this, Lucas: people who are desperate do desperate things. And I understand that. But—"

Lucas interrupted with another thought. "Doc, what about the signs that Thomas Stukeley still lived? I saw them with my own eyes!"

Doc Beecher looked thoughtful. Then he asked, "What did you expect to see, Lucas?"

"I— Well . . ." Lucas hadn't thought about that. "Bones, I guess. Dried up, dead old bones! Like that," he added, pointing to the skull sitting on the shelf.

"It was November when Thomas died, as I recall," said Doc. "It is now, let me see, why, it's the seventh of March. Thomas's body has been in the ground just a little over three months now, Lucas. Three months, I might add, when the weather was quite cold. What does that suggest to you, lad?"

Lucas shrugged.

"I did not see Thomas, of course," said Doc, "but

what you have described is not surprising. It sounds to me like the normal condition of a body after an interment of that length of time, at this time of the year."

"Mr. Stukeley said there was 'living blood' in the heart," said Lucas.

"By which he means blood that is red and flowing, I take it," said Doc. "I don't know how to explain that, Lucas, other than to say that it does not mean Thomas was drawing blood from Sarah or any other living soul.

"In medical school we dissected many corpses, lad, and I saw many strange things that I cannot explain."

"Well, how do you explain Enoch Rood?" Lucas asked eagerly. "He's cured! What about the stories Mrs. Rood heard? People in other places have been cured, too. Lots of people."

"Lucas, in my experience, accounts like that have a way of growing bigger as they get passed along. They take on a life of their own. And, I'm afraid, the truth often suffers in the process." Doc sighed. "People like a good story, lad. Each teller of the tale adds a touch here, a detail there, all to make the tale more intriguing and pleasing to his listeners. And if the one telling the story and the folks listening all want very much for the tale to end a certain way, well, you see what can happen."

Lucas frowned. "Do you mean Mrs. Rood was lying? And Mr. Rood, when he told me of Enoch's cure?"

"No, I don't mean that at all," answered Doc

Beecher. "I've no doubt Mrs. Rood believed what she'd heard. She wanted to believe it, lad, do you see?"

"Well, sure," said Lucas. "Because it meant maybe Enoch would live, too. And he did!"

"Yes, perhaps he did," agreed Doc. "Or, God forbid that this be so, perhaps he was merely experiencing a brief respite. I've seen consumption patients who burn with a bright light, seeming to have recovered, just before their flame flickers and dies. But by the time that occurred, you see, word of his 'cure' would already have traveled far and wide."

Silently, Lucas puzzled over Doc's words. Could Enoch be dead now, after all? Lucas didn't believe it. "What of the successes Mrs. Rood heard of in Rhode Island?" he asked. "Seems like somebody must have been cured, to get the 'story' started in the first place."

"Perhaps such a coincidence did occur," said Doc. "But the significance of it was exaggerated, lad, because it's our nature to make connections, to try to understand what happens to us, and to think we can do something about it."

Lucas agreed with part of what Doc had said. Lucas had seen the helplessness of the Stukeleys, and their desperate need to do something to ward off death, and he'd felt that same strong desire himself.

But how could Doc be so sure about everything else? He didn't know the Roods or the other families from Rhode Island. He hadn't been with the Stukeleys when they had performed the cure, hadn't felt the hope and the powerful exhilaration, as Lucas had.

"I still believe Sarah Stukeley will live," said Lucas quietly.

Doc removed his spectacles and rubbed his eyes. "Oh, lad," he said, "I hope you're right."

Twelve

❦

Doc and Lucas did not speak about Sarah Stukeley again as the short, dark days of March passed. Lucas kept his thoughts to himself, certain that time would prove to Doc that what he and the Stukeleys had done was right.

Southwick suffered a spell of weather so numbingly cold that Doc and Lucas treated three cases of severely frostbitten fingers, toes, cheeks, and ears in just one week.

"Half the people in the village are coughing, sneezing, and suffering from chills, and they're the ones who are well enough to get up from their beds," Doc proclaimed one frigid afternoon.

Several days later, two men arrived at the door carrying the body of Algander Lee, who had been discovered, frozen solid, in the street outside the Boar's

Head Tavern. Algander had left the tavern the evening before, having had, in the words of the innkeeper, Horace Clark, more rum than was wise for a man half his age and twice his size. The unfortunate Algander had fallen over in the snowy street and, too drunk to rise, had simply fallen asleep, his stiffened fingers still grasping the handle of the jug, never again to awaken in this world.

It was the first time since Lucas's arrival that Doc had been called upon in his capacity as village undertaker. Most farm families, Doc explained, had their own small graveyards and handled their own affairs when it came to death. It was becoming more common for folks who lived in town to turn to an undertaker, such as Doc.

Algander, it turned out, was brought to Doc because he had no family, and no one knew what to do with him. Doc said he'd take care of Algander himself, and he paid for the plain pine coffin Algander was buried in, despite Mrs. Bunce's disapproval.

"He was a disgrace," she said.

"I knew Algander before he ruined himself with drink," Doc said quietly. "The man I used to know would have been shamed to think he'd come to such an undignified end. I'm glad that at least I can give him a decent burial."

Lucas listened, moved by Doc's kindness. Later, he noticed the gentleness and respect with which Doc prepared Algander's body for burial.

Algander Lee's funeral offered Parson Reynolds an ideal opportunity to warn against "the pernicious effects of demon alcohol." Mrs. Bunce, along with Parson Reynolds and several of the other ladies in town, was a member of the American Temperance Society and was pleased to report to Doc and Lucas at supper that evening that several more of the townsfolk had joined the society as a result of Algander's hapless end.

The next morning Doc announced, "Lucas, Clem Buell's wound has had two weeks to heal." He grimaced. "And Clem's had two weeks to cool down about losing the leg. Much as I hate to go all the way out there in this cold, I need to pay him a call and see how he's getting on. Can you get the wagon ready?"

"Sure, Doc," said Lucas.

When they entered Clem Buell's cabin, they found him sitting alone in the dark, dirty room. Nat was nowhere in sight.

"How's the leg, Clem?" asked Doc.

Clem's eyes glared from his sunken face. "Gone," he said. "Thanks to you."

Doc sighed. "Clem, I was sorry to have to take the leg. Surely you know I wouldn't have done it unless I had to. If you'd called for me sooner—"

"I never did call for you," Clem growled. "It was that witless nephew of mine did it."

"That witless nephew of yours saved your life," said Doc sternly, "and I hope you haven't been abusing him for his effort. Now, are you going to let me look at the leg?"

Buell didn't answer. Doc appeared to take that as permission. He untied the bottom of Clem's pants leg and rolled it up to expose the stump. Lucas was relieved to see that the man's upper leg had shrunk back to a normal size. He watched as Doc prodded the flesh above where the tar sealed off the wound.

"You're lucky, Clem," Doc said.

Buell snorted.

"It looks as if the rot has stopped spreading. It'll be a while yet before I can fit you with a wooden leg, but I can get one prepared ahead. If you'll let Lucas here help you stand, I'll be able to take a measurement."

Clem Buell sat unmoving while Lucas struggled to get him up and balanced on his one foot.

"Help the lad out, can't you, Clem?" said Doc.

But Clem remained uncooperative as Doc made measurements around the thigh and from the stump to the dirt floor, saying only, "Don't want no peg leg."

"You'll change your mind about that. How have you been making out with the crutch?" Doc asked.

"That confounded thing?" said Buell with disgust.

"It takes some getting used to," Doc said. "I'll be back in another couple weeks, Clem, and we'll see about fitting you with a new leg, how's that?"

Buell didn't answer. Seated again, he stared straight ahead without expression.

"We'll be going, I guess." Doc picked up his black bag and nodded to Lucas. "It's going to be all right, Clem," he added gently. "Give it some time."

As they drove away in the wagon Lucas asked, "Is he always so ornery?"

"Put yourself in his shoes, Lucas," answered Doc. "Right now Clem's not thinking about the fact that he's alive; he's mourning the loss of that leg. To him, the remedy seems more painful than what ailed him, and he holds me to blame." He took a weary breath. "We do our best, lad, but our patients don't have to like it, and they don't have to thank us for it, either."

Several days later, as Lucas swept the office and Doc sat working at his desk, James Freeman stopped by with a loaf of headcheese, which he handed to Doc. "That's by way of payment for that lucky shave and haircut you gave me," he said, smiling hugely.

Doc allowed as how he'd heard through the grapevine that Martha Pitcher and James were betrothed, but that he was happy to hear it was true. "And to think I'd always thought Martha had sound judgment and good taste. It must have been a powerful moon out that night to addle her wits," he teased.

"It was no moon, I'm telling you. It was my own smooth cheeks and curly locks that won her," said James.

"Don't you be telling Martha that I barbered you, then," answered Doc. "When she figures out she got a pig in a poke, I don't want her blaming me!"

James left, promising to bring Martha by for a visit sometime soon, and Doc turned to Lucas. Blowing on his fingers to warm them, he said, "I see you're keeping the fire going, lad, but it seems to make no difference with these temperatures. It's the coldest month of March we've had since I started keeping these records some sixteen years ago."

Lucas smiled. The previous evening, even Mrs. Bunce had agreed that the kitchen was too cold for bathing.

"Pull that chair over here and have a look," Doc continued. "You might find this interesting."

Lucas joined Doc at the desk, where the book Doc had been studying lay open. "In these columns I've recorded the date, the patient's name and age, the nature of the disease or ailment I was called to treat, particulars of weather, such as the temperature, and whether or not there was snow or rainfall, and other miscellaneous details such as the phase of the moon and what-have-you."

Lucas remembered that Doc had been about to show him the record books the day Lydia Stukeley arrived at the door. He looked, seeing such entries as:

Ida Hemstreet (26)—March 3, 1835—Set bone in foot (cow stepped on)—33 degrees F—old snow, 2–3 inches—quarter moon
Lucius Cadwell (57)—January 25, 1836—Bled, gave tonic and plaster for fever, chills, aches, catarrh —28 degrees F—blizzard, strong wind and snow— half-moon

Abigail Jones (baby)—September 7, 1838—
Stillborn—76 degrees F—sunny—three-quarter
moon

"Now, some ailments, such as broken bones or accidents like Clem's, seem to occur with the same frequency at all times of the year, in all sorts of weather, in every phase of the moon, you see," Doc explained.

"Bee sting, naturally, will occur in the planting and harvest season, when bees and people are out and about. Other kinds of sickness, consumption being an obvious example, appear to occur much more often during the winter months. See this . . . and this . . . and here . . ."

Doc was running his finger down the columns, pointing out the dates when "consumption" was listed as the patient's complaint. Lucas nodded. He could see that the first symptoms usually came, as Doc had said, during the months of December, January, and February, although treatment of the illness might continue for longer than a year. The person could die from consumption, it appeared, at any time. But, yes, it looked as if most people came down with it during the winter.

"What of it, Doc?" he asked. "What does it mean?"

Doc laughed. "You do get right to the point, don't you, lad? As to what it all means, the answer is *I don't know*. But it seems likely to me, and there are other doctors who share my opinion, that just as there is a relationship between summer and bee stings, there is a relationship between winter and certain disease processes, whether it be from the presence of snow or cold, or the short days and long nights, or something else that occurs during these dark, dreary months."

Lucas thought for a moment. "Since those who are undead make their visits during the night," he said, "then longer nights would give them more time to make others sick. Yes!" He continued excitedly. "So in the winter—" He stopped when he saw the look on Doc's face.

"Lucas," said Doc, "I was hoping you'd forgotten about that—that business, but it's plain that you have not. What I'm asking you, lad, is to set aside your thinking about Thomas Stukeley or anyone else coming back from the grave to cause ill to others. Just put it aside for now, and see if what I'm telling you makes better sense."

Lucas answered stiffly, "I'll try, sir."

"I'm thinking, Lucas, that you've shown a lot of promise in your time here as my apprentice," Doc said. "I've found myself hoping you'll continue in the study of medicine."

Lucas shifted in his chair. He was pleased by the praise, but still angry at Doc's refusal to believe that Lucas understood what had made Sarah Stukeley ill, and what had cured her.

"But, Lucas, if you're to pursue this course of study

it is my responsibility to instill in you a scientific way of thinking. The study of medicine is progressing quickly, lad. I believe that someday, not in my lifetime, but perhaps in yours, we will understand the mysteries of consumption and many other diseases. But we cannot let ourselves be distracted by false ways of thinking.

"Now, you are looking for cause and effect in the case of Sarah Stukeley's disease, and you're right to do that, lad, with any illness.

"Example: A bee stings you. It causes you to have pain, swelling, itching, trouble breathing in some cases. The bee sting is the cause and the pain is the effect. But suppose that at the same moment the bee stung you a rooster crowed. Would you be correct in saying that the rooster's crow caused your pain and discomfort? The next time a rooster crowed, would you have the same symptoms?"

Lucas couldn't help grinning at Doc's suggestion. " 'Course not," he said.

Doc smiled, too. He continued enthusiastically. "Now, suppose you never saw the bee but you did hear the rooster. Do you see how you just might be fooled into thinking it was the rooster that caused your symptoms?"

Lucas laughed. "What if the sun came out at the same time? You might say the sun was the culprit, but you'd be wrong!"

"Exactly, lad!" Doc exclaimed, pounding his fist on

the desk. "So, you see, a true scientist will put his theories to the test time and time again to see if they hold up. In that way, he would prove that each time a bee stings, it causes certain effects to follow, but those same effects do not follow the crowing of the rooster. He can, therefore, eliminate the rooster as the cause of his discomfort."

"But everybody knows roosters don't sting, Doc," said Lucas.

"Aaah, then, let me choose a less obvious example," said Doc, rubbing his chin with relish. "Let us consider a case in which—"

Doc looked up as the door opened slightly and Lydia Stukeley's face appeared. Her cheeks were red from the cold, and her dark eyes shone brightly with some strong emotion. "Good day, Dr. Beecher. Good day to you, too, Lucas," she said.

"Come in, come in, Lydia," said Doc. "What brings you out on a cold day like this?"

"It's Sarah," cried Lydia excitedly.

There was a moment of silence while Lucas's heart thumped with anticipation. He was almost afraid to ask. "Sarah," he repeated cautiously.

"Oh, lass," said Doc, "is she—"

"She is well! She has recovered." Lydia's voice rose, trembling with joy. "Lucas! *Sarah is cured!*"

Thirteen

❧❧❧

That evening, Lucas, Doc Beecher, and Mrs. Bunce were in the kitchen sharing their evening meal when they heard a loud banging at the door to Doc's office. Lucas went to see who it was, and found a man who introduced himself as William Sheldon.

"I came to see Doc Beecher," he said. Looking at the man's face, Lucas was reminded of Lydia Stukeley's expression that afternoon. This man, too, appeared to be filled with some strong feeling.

"Come with me," said Lucas. "Doc's back here, in the kitchen."

"Good evening, William," said Mrs. Bunce when she saw their visitor.

"Sit, William, sit," said Doc, pulling out a chair. "How is Lavinia? I've been meaning to get out to see how she's coming along, but this blasted cold weather has made a coward of me, I'm afraid."

William Sheldon remained standing. He had removed his hat, and Lucas noticed that he was twisting it nervously in his hands.

"Will you join us in some supper?" asked Doc.

"No, thank you, Doc," he said. "I can't stay. I only came to ask—" He stopped, took a deep breath, and began again. "I know you heard about how the Stukeley girl was cured. The whole town's heard about it by now, I reckon. There's a good number of folks who've got family sick and dying of consumption—" Here his voice came near to breaking, and he stopped to swallow before continuing. "Like Lavinia, Doc. She's worse than ever."

"I'm sorry to hear that, William," said Doc.

"Lewis Stukeley's been telling all around town the way he dug up his son Thomas and took his heart, and how Sarah breathed the smoke from burning it, and how it cured her. And some of us got to talking at Talbot's store and we thought—"

Mrs. Bunce's hands had risen slowly from her lap to her own heart. "What are you saying? What?" She stopped. Her face looked deathly pale in the lamplight.

Doc Beecher reached across the table and took one of her hands and held it. "I'll explain in a moment, Cora," he said. "Let's hear William out."

"I guess Mrs. Stukeley found out about the cure from

kinfolk someplace. When Lewis Stukeley spoke of it at the store, Isaac Talbot said he'd heard of something like that from a traveler who passed through here a while back. This fellow told of a village in Vermont where folks gathered on the green for a curing ceremony. They burned the hearts of the undead ones right there on the blacksmith's anvil. The man told Isaac it was the end of consumption in the village."

"Undead ones?" Mrs. Bunce repeated in a quavering voice. "Uriah, what do you know about this?"

"I've heard some talk of it," answered Doc Beecher. Turning once again to William Sheldon, he asked, "Why have you come to see me, William?"

Sheldon shifted uncomfortably and twisted his hands tighter around his hat. "We're spreading the word to all whose families are afflicted with the consumption, Doc. And those that wish to benefit from the remedy will meet tomorrow in the town square. In that town in Vermont I guess there was some doctors from the local medical college who helped out, and we were hoping— Well, folks asked would I see if you'd attend and do whatever you can. We'd like your boy here, who's had some experience from the sounds of it, to come as well."

"I'm sorry to hear that Lavinia is doing poorly," said Doc. "If I thought that what you're suggesting would help her, or any of the others who are ill, I'd be the first to join you. But I don't hold with the practice you're speaking of. It's superstition, pure and simple, William."

Lucas had been listening with growing dismay. He could contain himself no longer. "But, Doc, Sarah Stukeley! She was cured!" he cried.

"Remember our talk this afternoon?" Doc asked quietly. "What you're hearing is the rooster crowing, lad."

Mrs. Bunce stared from one to the other as if they all had taken leave of their senses.

William Sheldon was looking down at his hat, trying to poke it back into shape for wearing. "Doc, those medicines you gave me for Lavinia aren't helping. She's . . . dying."

Doc's face was in shadow, but Lucas thought he'd never heard such pain and sorrow as was in Doc's voice when he answered. "I'm truly sorry, William. But there's nothing else I can do."

"I got to try this, Doc," said William Sheldon. His eyes, suddenly filled with tears, looked pleadingly at Doc.

"I know," said Doc softly. "I know."

There was an awkward silence. "I'll be going, then," said Sheldon.

"I shall pray for Lavinia, William," said Doc. "But I won't be at the square tomorrow." As Sheldon turned to leave, Doc added, "And neither will the lad."

No one at the table said a word as the sound of William Sheldon's footsteps faded down the hallway.

When the door closed behind him, Mrs. Bunce spoke. "Well. What on earth was that about, Uriah? It sounds as if the entire town has gone mad!"

"No, Cora, not mad. But they're caught up in a powerful spell," said Doc. "And I'm afraid they're in for a bitter disappointment."

Lucas sat fidgeting anxiously while Doc explained to Mrs. Bunce about the cure. When Doc paused for a moment, Lucas couldn't help himself. "Sarah Stukeley *was* cured, Mrs. Bunce. I was there."

Cora Bunce drew in her breath sharply.

"And I want to be at the town square tomorrow, too," Lucas said.

"You'll do no such thing," Mrs. Bunce declared firmly. "The idea of an apprentice to Dr. Beecher taking part in such nonsense! Why, people would think Uriah approved."

Lucas appealed to Doc. "Mr. Sheldon thinks I can help!"

"Just what is it you can do to assist, lad?" asked Doc.

"I—I don't know exactly," Lucas admitted. "But, well, it seems like neighbors should help each other out when there's trouble. Or at least try," he added.

Doc Beecher sighed. "Even when no good will come of it?" he asked.

"I don't know that!" cried Lucas. "And I don't see how you can be so sure you're right!" He stared down at the table, trying to control the rapid beating of his heart. He hadn't meant to talk rudely to Doc, who had shown him nothing but kindness. Still . . .

Then, to his surprise, Doc said quietly, "All right, lad. Go to the town square tomorrow. Help if you can."

"Uriah!" Mrs. Bunce said, frowning at her brother in irritation.

"Now get along to bed," Doc went on, looking at Lucas. "It's been a tiring day."

Lucas got up slowly from the table. "Thank you, Doc," he whispered. As he walked past the parlor to his room, he heard Mrs. Bunce's indignant voice. "Uriah, what can you be thinking of? The whole business is ridiculous."

And Doc's melancholy reply: "Yes, Cora. But it gives me no pleasure to know that."

Fourteen

Lucas lay on the bed, his eyes wide open, his thoughts racing. He tried to be still, but his body felt prickly and jumpy. He was eager for the morning to come, for the ceremony to take place at the town square, for the sick to be cured, and for Doc to see that Lucas had been right.

When the first frail light began to show in the eastern sky, Lucas could lie in bed no longer. He rose, did every task he could think of to please Mrs. Bunce, and then, quietly, he left by the kitchen door.

The town was just beginning to come awake as he walked down the still dark main street. Windows brightened as candles and lamps were lit; the smell of wood smoke drifted through the air. Lucas smelled biscuits baking and tried to ignore his hunger.

When Lucas arrived at the deserted town square, he found a spot out of the wind and waited. The day, which had started out bright and clear, turned dark and dreary by early afternoon, when the first townsfolk appeared at the square. The snow and ice had melted, and the road was muddy and filled with deep ruts. A cold drizzle began to fall, making the footing even more perilous. Lucas stood with his hands in his pockets and his shoulders hunched, watching.

William Sheldon was one of the first to arrive. Behind him in the wagon, bundled against the damp chill under layers of quilts, lay a woman Lucas guessed was his wife, Lavinia. William turned to her and spoke, and Lucas heard her cough weakly in response.

More people came, struggling through the mud and rain, some on foot, some on horseback, others, as sick as Lavinia Sheldon, lying in the backs of wagons. Most were strangers to Lucas, but he saw a few people he knew. Eben Oaks, James Freeman, and several other men were carrying wood and stacking it in a pyramid-shaped pile in the center of the square. Daniel and Mrs. Oaks stood huddled by the door of the blacksmith shop, trying to keep warm. The Stukeley family pulled up in their wagon and Lucas went to greet them.

As he made his way through the thickening crowd, he overheard bits of conversation and snatches of hushed voices.

"—hasn't been a case of consumption in Vermont since they—"

"—see Sarah Stukeley?"

"—the very picture of health."

Lucas smiled, looking over toward Sarah. Though still pale and thin, she was smiling brightly and talking to the well-wishers who gathered around the wagon. Continuing to push past groups of townspeople to get to the Stukeleys, Lucas couldn't help but hear more of the talk. He felt his neck flush when someone whispered, "There's Doc Beecher's apprentice. He's the one who saved the Stukeley girl."

"They say he's cured lots of others . . ."

"I heard that when they opened Thomas Stukeley's coffin, Thomas sat right up and opened his eyes!"

"Yes, and his heart was filled with fresh blood."

"It poured right out of his mouth—"

"He screamed when they cut into him—"

"—like to make your hair curl—"

Lucas listened uneasily, his smile turning to a frown. He wanted to stop and say, "That's not the way it happened," but he felt shy about talking to people he didn't know, who, after all, hadn't been talking to him. He walked on, shaking his head, wondering where people had heard such things. It reminded him of something Doc had said.

At that moment, Lydia looked up and saw him, and he forgot everything else. "Lucas!" she called happily. "Look! Here's Sarah."

Lucas said hello to Sarah, Lydia, and Samuel. Then, turning back to Sarah, he added, "You're looking fit as a fiddle." It was an expression he'd heard Doc use. Sarah beamed.

"But you, Lucas," said Lydia, "look frozen stiff. Get up here in the wagon under the blankets. We've brought hot cider and some biscuits, too. Would you like some?"

Gratefully, Lucas sipped the cider and munched on a biscuit, snuggling under the warm wool coverlet with Lydia, Sarah, and young Samuel Stukeley. The sky grew darker, and a chilly wind blew from the northwest. Parson Reynolds arrived and stood by while the final sticks of wood were placed on the pile.

Lucas, his hunger satisfied for the moment, looked about him. Usually when so many people gathered together there was a mood of merriment. But the atmosphere on the square was not like that at a husking bee, or a wedding, or a dance. People's faces were grave, their voices hushed. Occasionally, the sound of agonized coughing carried on the wind. It was like being in church, Lucas thought.

And, indeed, at that moment, Parson Reynolds began to speak. "We are gathered here, my friends, in the eyes of Almighty God, to bring about the healing of our brothers and sisters stricken with the scourge of consumption. We have witnessed the miraculous recovery of one of our flock, Miss Sarah Stukeley, and recognize that God the Father works in mysterious ways which are not always given us to understand.

"We come in faith and hope. We come in the

110

knowledge that God helps those who help themselves. We thank those who have led us to this cure, that we may use it to help our loved ones. May God bless us and our endeavor. Let us pray."

All bowed their heads in prayer, their voices murmuring along with that of Parson Reynolds. Then Lewis Stukeley rose to speak.

In a voice so low the crowd had to strain to hear it above the wind, Mr. Stukeley said, "I am a simple, God-fearing man. I watched three of my children die. I tried to tell myself it was God's will. But why, I asked myself, would God want my babies to die. I could find no answer.

"Anna and I, we tried everything we knew and everything Doc Beecher knew to do, but nothing helped. And so when I heard tell of this cure we're about to perform, I knew I had to try and save our Sarah. And, by God, she was saved!"

Heads turned toward them, and people nodded and smiled at Sarah. Lucas heard murmurs: "Praise God" and "Amen." Then, to Lucas's surprise, Lewis Stukeley pointed to him.

"Young Lucas Whitaker there, the one in the wagon with my family, he helped. He'd heard of the cure, too, where he came from. Folks in Vermont and Rhode Island, some say even as far away as Maine, have put an end to this sickness. And that's why we're here, to do the same.

"Those of you who have sick ones in the family were

told what you needed to do before you came here to-day. We're going to light this fire now, and those of you with—with something to place upon it, come on up here. When it's burning good, we'll let the sickest folks be brought up first, to breathe in the smoke, before we take our turns. Afterward, those who want some of the ashes are welcome to 'em."

Lewis nodded to Eben Oaks, who set the pile of logs alight. There was a long moment when no one moved. Everyone stared, transfixed, as the fire crackled to life. Then, slowly, one by one, people began to come forward.

It gave Lucas a peculiar feeling to see the offerings they held carefully in their hands. The bundles were covered in cloth, or placed in boxes of wood or containers of tin, or, in one case, wrapped in dried husks of corn. The packages contained the hearts of family members who had been buried.

As the bundles were fed to the flames, Lucas touched his own heart and thought that if he were the one returning to make folks sick, he'd want someone to stop him. Likely these souls, too, wished to be put to rest.

Lucas had never before been part of something so big and important, and his throat felt thick, as if he were about to cry. He watched as William Sheldon carried his wife, Lavinia, in his arms, carried her close to the smoke from the blazing fire. A look of rapture passed over her face as she took the cure, breathing deeply once, twice, three times, of the life-saving smoke.

Lucas looked at William's face. It, too, shone radiantly in the light from the fire. He looked around at all the people gathered in the square and saw the same glowing look of hope and expectation, and felt his own face transformed by it, too. He felt dazed and overwhelmed, as if his body couldn't contain the powerful, mysterious feelings he had inside.

By the time Lucas and the Stukeleys went forward to pass slowly by the fire, an early darkness had begun to creep across the village square. People stood in the gathering dusk, watching the last embers of the fire flicker and fade. Then quietly, solemnly, they collected ashes to take with them.

The wind had died down, and a few stars peeked down from the blue-black sky. Lucas walked back to the wagon with the Stukeleys, and helped Lydia up onto the seat. "I'm glad you came today, Lucas," she said.

"I'm glad, too," Lucas answered truthfully, adding, "I hope to see you soon."

"Yes," said Lydia, smiling. "I hope so. Good night, Lucas."

Lucas said goodbye to the Stukeleys and stood waving until their wagon was out of sight. He looked around and saw that he was the only person left at the square. The fire had burned down to a faint reddish glow.

Still full of the power and mystery of the ceremony, Lucas began to walk slowly back to Doc's house. He wanted to hold on to the feeling of awe and certainty as long as he could, and he didn't know which was going to be harder to face, Doc's kindly skepticism or the scorn and disapproval of Mrs. Bunce.

Fifteen

∽᧞◡᧞◠

When Lucas stepped into the kitchen, Doc was sitting at the table sipping tea. He offered Lucas some soup, and Lucas sat down to join him.

"Where's Mrs. Bunce?" asked Lucas, thinking that if she was going to question him about the curing, he'd just as soon get it over with.

But Doc answered, "Her rheumatism was acting up. She took to her bed early."

Relieved, Lucas sipped his soup, grateful for its warmth. He waited for Doc to ask about the ceremony, but Doc said nothing about it. Instead, he asked, "Do you remember when we spoke about Moll Garfield, lad?"

Lucas was surprised. "The witch?" he asked. "I mean, the granny woman?"

"Yes," said Doc.

"Sure," said Lucas.

"Well, there's something I'd like you to do for me," Doc went on. "You know I send to Philadelphia for most of my medicines, but a good many of them I make up from herbs and plants I get from Moll. I'd like you to go there to replenish my supplies of certain items. That will be one reason for your visit."

"What's the other reason?" Lucas asked.

"Well, you see, I've intended to pay her a call to see how she's fared over this long, blasted cold spell, but, what with one thing and another, I haven't gotten to it. So I want you to go and make sure she's all right. And that's the tricky part, lad. She can't know that's what you're doing."

Lucas raised his eyebrows questioningly.

"Moll's a proud old girl," explained Doc. "Keeps herself to herself and has never needed or asked for help from anyone. She still chops and hauls all her own firewood, hunts or grows all her food, not to mention gathering and digging her plants and roots. I'm sure she's made it through the winter better than most. But I'll feel more peaceful in my mind knowing for sure."

"What will I say to her?" asked Lucas cautiously.

"I'll give you a list of supplies that I need. Tell her you're my apprentice. Tell her I want you to learn some of the old Pequot healing secrets," he added with a twinkle in his eye. "And, meanwhile, keep a sharp eye out."

"For what?"

"Anything that needs doing. If the roof was leaking—"

"I could fix it, I guess," said Lucas.

"That's the idea. If she'll let you." Doc laughed. "And if she hasn't already done it herself."

Lucas frowned. "But how long do you want me to stay?"

"That depends," Doc said cheerfully. "As long as you need to."

"What about my chores?" Lucas asked. "What about helping you and Mrs. Bunce?"

"We'll just have to manage without you for a time, lad," said Doc. "Don't you worry about us."

Lucas sat quietly for a moment. All the exhilaration he'd felt earlier was gone. "Is it because I went to the curing today?" he asked. "Is that why you're sending me away?"

"What?" exclaimed Doc. "I gave you permission to go to the town square, lad. No one is punishing you for it."

Lucas remained still, staring down at his empty cup.

"Lucas, look at me," said Doc. "I'm not sending you away. Not the way you're meaning it. I'm asking a favor. A favor to me and a stubborn old woman."

Lucas didn't answer, and Doc gazed searchingly at him. Then he smiled, as if he'd thought of something. "There's no harm in Moll, Lucas, if that's what you're thinking."

Lucas looked up into Doc's clear blue eyes.

"All right," Doc said ruefully. "I can see there's no hiding the truth from you. There's more to it than I've been telling you. You see, lad, the fact is, I'm thinking you need a little time away from here, away from all your chores and responsibilities.

"You buried your mother and came here . . . And I can tell you truly that I'm glad for the day when you appeared at my door." He smiled. "But it strikes me you haven't had much time to catch your breath.

"So go to Moll, lad. I believe you'll find her to be easy company. I need the supplies, and I'm also thinking you two can do each other some good. Whenever you're ready, come on back. Mrs. Bunce and I aren't going anywhere."

Later, in bed, Lucas thought about visiting Moll Garfield. If Doc wanted him to go, of course he'd go. Doc said there was no harm in the woman, and Lucas supposed he believed it. He even smiled a bit in the darkness, thinking about what Lydia Stukeley would say if she knew he was going to stay in the little cabin with the "witch woman."

Sixteen

After working all morning under the scowling super-vision of Mrs. Bunce, Lucas felt almost relieved to be walking out of town on his own. Near dusk, he found himself in the clearing outside Moll Garfield's house. The yellow glow of candlelight shone from the window of her cabin, and Lucas could smell the smoke from the fire. He was lingering at the edge of the woods, unsure of what to do next, when the cabin door slowly opened.

Moll Garfield stood in the doorway, staring in Lucas's direction. His approach had been silent and he had not yet left the cover of the trees, but the woman seemed to know he was there. Although her figure was lit from behind, leaving her face in shadow, Lucas felt her eyes holding his in a steady gaze.

He jumped, startled, as the sudden tremulous hooting

of an owl broke the silence: *Hoo, hoo-hoo, hoo, hoo*. Its large, dark shape floated across the clearing.

"Come in, child," said Moll. Her voice sounded hoarse and rusty, like the creaking of an old gate in the wind.

Slowly, Lucas walked forward. As he followed Moll into the little house, he sniffed deeply of the pleasant, powerful smell that greeted his nostrils. Bunches of dried herbs hung from the roof beams and on the walls, along with bundles of the roots and stalks and bulbs of many different plants. Their exotic odors mingled with the familiar aromas of food cooking, wood burning, and beeswax dripping from the single candle that lit the room.

The candle flame flickered and a log sputtered in the fire, drawing Lucas's attention back to the woman, who was now sitting before the hearth. Her straight black hair was streaked with gray and hung down her back in a long braid.

"Sit," she said simply.

When Lucas hesitated, she motioned for him to take a place by the fire. He sat on the rough plank floor, his back to the hearth, and looked up into the face of Moll Garfield.

Deep wrinkles lined her dark brown skin. Her nose jutted forward, strong and distinct, between high sharp cheekbones. Holding a clay pipe clamped between her teeth, she squinted at him through the smoke that rose lazily from the bowl. She didn't say anything. It seemed to him that she was learning things about him by looking, instead of by asking questions, the way most people did.

The long silence made Lucas uneasy. He thought he should say something. "I'm Lucas Whitaker," he offered. "Doc Beecher sent me. I'm his apprentice, you see, and he needs—" Lucas fumbled in the pocket of his coat for the list of supplies Doc wanted.

Moll shook her head. "There's time for that later," she said. Gently, she reached out and laid both hands on Lucas's cheeks. Her fingers were dry and cool. She moved them slowly over his face, feeling his forehead, eyebrows, lips, ears, chin, and finally, very slowly, her palms traced the shape of his head. At last, she appeared satisfied.

She took the pipe from her mouth and spoke in her rusty voice. "You are young, but you have seen much trouble."

Lucas felt a lump rise in his throat. Moll rose from her chair and took the kettle of hot water from the fire. Lucas watched as she measured out portions of several different herbs and made tea. She returned to her chair with a steaming cup, which she handed to Lucas. "Here," she said. "Drink this."

Lucas sniffed the heady, pungent smell of the tea, then tried a cautious sip. It was rich and sweet and soothing. He drank again. Moll sat quietly in her chair, watching the fire. She seemed to accept Lucas's presence without question, and he felt himself begin to relax. The combined warmth from the tea and the fire crept through his body and into his bones, and his eyes began to close.

Dimly, he became aware of Moll moving quietly about the room. The cup was taken from his hand, blankets were placed gently over him, and the candle was extinguished. Darkness came, and sleep.

When daylight touched his eyelids, he awoke. He was lying still, looking around the cabin and trying to remember where he was and how he'd come to be there, when Moll Garfield walked through the door. She filled a pot with water, carried it over to where Lucas lay by the hearth, and began poking the ashes to life.

Turning to Lucas, she smiled, her face creasing into deeper wrinkles. "Sleep well, did you?" she asked.

Lucas yawned and stretched. It was the deepest, most peaceful sleep he'd had in a long time. Since before Mama died, he realized. "Yes, ma'am," he answered.

Moll glanced at him from the corners of her eyes. "Moll will do, thank you kindly," she said. She fed some small sticks to the embers and blew on them to coax a flame to life. Lucas studied her as she added larger sticks and, finally, three logs to the fire. Her features revealed her Pequot ancestry, but he couldn't say that he saw anything witchlike about her.

As to her health and how she'd fared over the winter, Lucas thought, Doc could set his mind at ease. Moll looked strong and sprightly as she moved about the room, preparing food for their breakfast. She turned to Lucas, nodding with satisfaction, and said, "Camomile, motherwort, skullcap, and lady's slipper."

Lucas was confused. "Beg your pardon?"

"The tea," Moll answered. "It helped you to sleep."

Lucas remembered the sweet, strong taste of the drink Moll had given him. He looked around at all the herbs and plants, and wondered at their uses. At the same time he kept an eye out, as Doc had told him to do, for anything amiss, but the little cabin appeared snug and sound.

"Would you show me how to make it?" Lucas asked shyly. "Doc said to ask if you'd teach me things."

Moll took a taste from the pot she was stirring. "First," she said, "you must eat."

At the mention of food, Lucas's stomach rumbled loudly. Moll laughed, a startling sound like the cawing of a crow. She filled two dishes, handed one to Lucas, and began eating, smacking her lips with satisfaction.

When they finished, Moll took him deep into the woods, where she showed him where to look for the mosses, barks, and tender sprouts that could be gathered in early spring. As they walked along, she pointed out places where, later in the season, leaves and flowers and berries of healing plants would appear in abundance.

Lucas loved hearing their names: cocklebur, sticklewort, coltsfoot, knitbone, blowball, feverfew, bearberry, toadflax, heart's ease. He repeated them to himself, trying to remember which ones Moll used for cough, or fever, which for toothache, or burns, or wounds.

Later, while Moll prepared the evening meal, Lucas looked around. There was a large, neatly stacked supply of firewood, and a patch of new shingles on the roof. Moll did, indeed, appear to be doing just fine by herself.

As they sat by the hearth eating, Lucas said, "Moll?" At first he had felt odd calling her by the familiar name, but he'd soon become used to it. "What do you know about—consumption?"

Moll grunted and spat into the fire. Looking at Lucas from under her hooded eyelids, she said, "I know that after the white man's ships came, many, many of my mother's people died from it. From red spot. And from other diseases." Her voice grew bitter. "My mother knew the remedies for illness. She learned them from her mother and she taught them to me. But there was no remedy for the white man's sicknesses."

"Your mother's people," repeated Lucas. "The Pequots."

Moll looked surprised. "Yes," she said. Her eyes looked somewhere far away, somewhere Lucas couldn't see.

Finally, he said, "Moll, there is a cure for consumption."

Moll's face lost its look of sad remembrance and she gave a snort of laughter. "What has that old gray fox Beecher been telling you, child?"

"Doc didn't tell me," said Lucas.

Moll lifted her eyebrows. Again he had the feeling she was seeing past his face and into the hidden places inside. That made it easy to tell her about the deaths of his family, about digging up Thomas Stukeley's grave and putting him to rest so that Sarah would live, and about the curing ceremony he had attended at the town square.

While he talked, Moll filled her pipe with tobacco and lit it. When Lucas finished, she peered at him through the smoke. "Ah, but how does this story end?" she asked.

What did Moll mean, Lucas wondered. What he'd been telling her wasn't a story. It was true. And he had told her everything. It ended in Southwick, with the ceremony at the town square. It ended with Enoch Rood and Sarah Stukeley and Lavinia Sheldon, and all the others, cured. It ended with the end of consumption!

"Sometimes," Moll said, glancing slyly at Lucas, "you must go back to the beginning of the story to find out how it ends."

Lucas didn't know how to respond. Maybe Moll wasn't a witch, but she certainly had some strange ways about her, he thought.

Seventeen

꧁꧂

On days when a chilly spring rain was falling, Lucas and Moll spent their time indoors. Moll went through her stores of plants and explained their uses to Lucas, and how best to prepare them.

When the weather was fair, they roamed the woods together. Lucas, who had spent his entire life in the Connecticut countryside, felt as if he were seeing it for the first time. Moll pointed out the dens of foxes and bears, the holes where woodchucks had slept the winter months away, the matted grassy spots where deer had bedded down, the places where their fawns had been born.

Sometimes people stopped by for medicines or advice. Lucas watched and listened as Moll dispensed black walnut hulls for tapeworm, catnip for colic, angelica root for rheumatism, peppermint and ginger to ease stomach pain, thyme and spearmint to freshen the breath, honey to sweeten the disposition. One day Moll sent Lucas to gather cobwebs, which she used to bandage the wound on a young girl's leg.

Lucas noticed that the leaves and bark from the slippery elm were Moll's favorite remedy for sore throats and cough. She even made ointments out of the sap, which she used for burns and cuts. Lucas tried to remember everything, so he could ask Doc about it when he returned.

Lucas liked being with Moll. She didn't speak unless she had something to say, and much of their time was spent in a companionable silence. Sometimes, with a guilty pang, Lucas thought that he should leave and go back to Doc's. Moll was teaching him things, yes, which was partly why Doc had sent Lucas to her. But as for the rest, Lucas had seen from the start that Moll didn't need any help from him. Still, for some reason Lucas couldn't explain to himself, he wasn't ready to return to Doc's.

He had a lot of time to reflect on all that had happened. Bothersome thoughts and questions buzzed around his head in the pesky manner of summer flies. They were distracting and annoying, and he couldn't quite grasp them.

He remembered the whispered remarks at the curing ceremony, and the way people were saying that Thomas

Stukeley had sat up in the coffin, screaming, with blood pouring from his mouth. It was all wrong. Lucas kept hearing Doc's words about the way tales got bigger as they were passed from one person to the next. How many mouths had passed the stories of the cure from Rhode Island and Vermont to far-off Connecticut, he wondered. How much had each of them shaped the story, changing what really happened?

And it was disturbing that Moll had laughed when he'd told her there was a cure for consumption. True, she had listened as Lucas told her about it, but then she had asked how the story ended.

Most of all, it bothered him that Doc thought the cure was nonsense. Doc was smart, and if Doc didn't believe, well . . . Now that Lucas had time alone to think, he found himself questioning things that only a week before he had believed with all his heart.

Buzzzz . . . Buzzzz . . . Buzzzz . . . The irksome questions swarmed about in his brain. He grew more and more restless, like a baby bird eager to peck its way out of the egg, or a snake itching to shed its winter skin.

He had been with Moll a little over a week when he awakened one morning to a shrill *cock-a-doodle-doo*! But, he thought groggily, Moll didn't keep chickens. Still muddled with sleep, Lucas puzzled about it until he realized that he'd been dreaming.

The dream made him think of Doc, and he tried to

figure out why. Then he remembered. In his mind he heard Doc's voice: "What you're hearing is the rooster crowing, lad."

Lucas opened his eyes, fully awake. Doc had said those words when William Sheldon came to the house, right after Lucas insisted that he and the Stukeleys had cured Sarah.

He lay still for a long time, pondering his dream and the meaning behind Doc's words. He asked himself: Had he been fooled by the rooster's crowing? Was Sarah Stukeley still well? Was Lavinia Sheldon feeling better? Did Enoch truly recover? He had to know.

Moll came inside then, holding a basket filled with green stalks that curled delicately at the ends. She placed them in a pot of water and started them boiling over the fire. After just a few moments, she filled a dish from the pot and handed it to Lucas. He took a mouthful of the greens. They were tender and mild and the taste made him think of summer. Moll was watching him closely.

"Good," he said, taking another mouthful.

"They're the first new shoots of fiddlehead fern," Moll informed him. "Found 'em this morning. And that means winter's back is broken."

Could the long, cold winter be ending at last, Lucas wondered. He stood up, opened the door, stepped out into the clearing, and sniffed the air. Beneath the morning chill, he could feel a touch of warmth in the pale sunlight, and he could smell the wormy, rich aroma of earth.

With surprise, Lucas realized that March had turned to April. Some knowledge deep in their roots had told the ferns it was time to poke their delicate heads up through the damp, soft earth. It struck Lucas as a brave and reckless thing to do, and he smiled at the notion.

As he and Moll ate their morning meal, he told her he'd be leaving that day, and thanked her for allowing him to stay. She nodded, then helped him to wrap up the supplies Doc had asked for.

When he was ready to go, she walked with him to the edge of the clearing. Lucas swallowed. "You said that sometimes a person has to go back to the beginning of a story to find out how it ends," he said.

Moll nodded and reached out to touch his shoulder. Then she turned back to the little cabin, and Lucas headed off through the woods. Not south to town, but north, toward his family's farm.

Eighteen

❧

It was late, and very dark, when Lucas knocked at the door of the Roods' farmhouse. There were murmurs of surprise and confusion as the family awakened from sleep. Soon a candle was lit and Lucas heard footsteps approaching.

Oliver Rood spoke through the door. "Who's that?"

"It's me, Mr. Rood. Lucas Whitaker."

"Lucas!" The door flew open. Mr. Rood stood in his long johns, thrusting the candle into Lucas's face. "By God, it *is* you." He stared at Lucas, his eyes wide, his face pale, as if he saw a ghost. "Mary!" he called. "It's Lucas Whitaker, as I live and breathe."

Mrs. Rood came to the door in her nightdress, her face showing the same startled expression as her husband's. "Lord be praised, Lucas," she said wonderingly.

"We'd given you up for lost. Thank God you're here and well!"

Sleepy voices called from the back room, and Mrs. Rood went to soothe the children. Lucas and Mr. Rood sat at the table, and soon Mrs. Rood returned to join them.

"We worried so about you, Lucas," she said. "Where have you been?"

Lucas felt ashamed. He'd never thought to send word to the Roods to tell them where he was, or that he was alive. "I'm sorry," he said. "I never thought—I've been living in Southwick—"

"Southwick!" exclaimed Mrs. Rood. "Why?"

"I found work there," said Lucas. A note of pride entered his voice as he explained. "I stay with Dr. Uriah Beecher. I'm his apprentice."

"Well, that's fine, Lucas," said Mr. Rood slowly. "We did kindly wonder where you'd got to. We've been in a muddle about what to do with the farm and all."

"I was glad to know you had the use of the animals," said Lucas.

Mrs. Rood said, "That Ruth's a real good milker."

Quietly, Lucas asked, "Barnabas and Reuben and Rachel, have they been working hard for Enoch?"

In the strained silence that followed, Lucas felt his heart sink. Mr. and Mrs. Rood exchanged uneasy glances. At last Mr. Rood said, "Enoch passed away, Lucas." His expression tightened with grief. "He died not long after you left."

It was what Lucas had come to find out. It was what he'd feared he would discover. Nevertheless, there was a plunging feeling in his stomach, and he had to struggle to breathe.

"He *was* better, Lucas," said Mrs. Rood. Tears filled her eyes in a sudden rush. "We were so sure. And then he took a turn for the worse. It happened so fast—"

"Something went amiss with his cure," said Mr. Rood. "It was working so good and then—"

"We sent word to my kinfolk in Rhode Island, asking what to do," said Mrs. Rood, "but we haven't heard back yet." In the light from the candle her face was lined and careworn. "I pray they hasten with their reply . . . in time to save Matthew."

From the back room came the sound of coughing. "Mama?" a voice called weakly. Mrs. Rood stood up. "I'll go see to him," she said. "Lucas, Mr. Rood will show you where to sleep." She smiled. "We're glad to have you."

Mr. Rood was pacing the rough plank floor. "I've been talking to folks, Lucas. And I heard that it might be another one of the family coming back to bother Matthew. Mercy we put to rest, you know, but it could be one of the others. Maybe Enoch."

He stopped his pacing and turned to Lucas. "We've got to stop it."

"How do you mean to do that?" asked Lucas. But even as he asked, he knew.

"I aim to dig up all their graves. We'll find which

one still lives. We'll be able to tell, you know, by the signs. And we'll end this for good and for all."

Lucas looked at Mr. Rood's haggard face, his desperate, pleading eyes. He felt an enormous sadness for Mr. and Mrs. Rood. Their bewilderment, their fear, their belief in the cure even in the face of Enoch's death—he understood it all.

"It's a blessing, you showing up like this, Lucas," said Mr. Rood. "I can sure use a hand in the morning. So you get some sleep now, hear?"

Mr. Rood returned to bed. Lucas sat down, holding his head in his hands. Enoch, his friend, was dead. And now Mr. Rood wanted Lucas's help in digging up more graves, including Enoch's. He tried to imagine working alongside Mr. Rood, pretending to believe that what they were doing would save Matthew.

How he wished Doc were there, so he could ask him what to do. But he knew what Doc would do. Now he understood how Doc must have felt facing the Stukeleys and William Sheldon, how difficult it must have been to refuse to help with the "cure." Doc had had the courage to tell the truth. And, cruel as it seemed to take away the Roods' only hope for Matthew, Lucas knew he would have to summon the same courage come morning.

He passed a fitful night by the hearth. When Mr. Rood awoke and came to stir the fire to life, Lucas sat up. "Mr. Rood?" he said.

"Good morning, Lucas. Did you sleep well?"

"Not so good, I guess," said Lucas. "I was thinking about Matthew and what you aim to do today."

"I confess it occupied my thoughts most of the night, as well," said Mr. Rood. "I'll be glad to get on with it."

"Do you remember I said I was working for a doctor?" Lucas asked.

"Uriah Beecher, did you say his name is?"

"Right."

Mr. Rood looked up with interest. "Has this Beecher told you anything about how to work the cure?"

"No," answered Lucas. He took a deep breath and went on. "In fact, he doesn't hold to it. He says sometimes folks get cured of consumption, but not because of digging up graves or any of that. He says the dead can't come back to hurt anybody."

Mr. Rood was listening intently. He thought for a moment, then asked eagerly, "These folks who do get well, how does he cure them?"

Lucas squirmed uncomfortably. "Well, he gives them plasters and medicines—"

"We've tried those things," said Mr. Rood impatiently.

"He says he doesn't know why some people get better," Lucas said softly. "And that anybody who says he knows isn't telling the truth."

"Doesn't sound like much of a doctor to me," Mr. Rood said angrily. "You're telling me he'd just stand by and do nothing?"

Before Lucas could answer, Mr. Rood went on.

"Well, I can't do that, by God. I've got to at least try the only thing I know to do!"

"I know, sir," said Lucas. "I—"

From the other room came the sounds of Mrs. Rood and the other children rising. Mr. Rood looked hard at Lucas. "Don't say a word about this to Mrs. Rood, do you hear? She holds out hope for this cure. I won't have you making her think she's going to lose Matthew, too."

"Yes, sir," said Lucas quietly.

"I'm going out there now to do what I have to do, Lucas, and I'm sorry you can't see your way to help out. I'm going to pray that you and that doctor of yours are wrong."

Lucas sat where he was. Mrs. Rood and the children soon joined him. While Mrs. Rood fixed biscuits, she and Lucas discussed arrangements for selling the farm. Lucas offered to sell the animals, too, and give the profit to the Roods in return for their caring for them over the winter. To his relief, Mrs. Rood said that Reuben, Rachel, Barnabas, and Ruth seemed like part of the family and she'd just as soon keep them.

Before he left to begin the three-mile walk to his own family farm, Lucas joined Mrs. Rood in a heartfelt prayer for Matthew's recovery.

Nineteen

❦

When Lucas stepped onto the land that he and Pa and Asa had cleared for the farm, a strange feeling swept over him. It seemed so long ago that he had lived here with his family. When he and Pa and Asa had hauled out rocks and tree stumps and prepared the stony ground for planting, Lucas had figured he'd stay on this land forever. Now the house, the fields, the animal sheds, and especially Mama's garden had a neglected, lonesome look.

He climbed the hill to the small graveyard. Pa's headstone had been heaved sideways by the winter frost, and Lucas straightened it. He touched the stones at each grave, and memories of his family flooded him. But they were not the awful memories that had been part of him for so long, of the slow wasting and weakening, the coughing and the pain.

Now he remembered Pa, strong and vigorous, urging Reuben and Rachel to pull one more time on a stubborn stump, and Pa's look of satisfaction when the job was done.

As if it were yesterday, he could see Lizy carrying a pitcher of buttermilk out to the field. He smiled, remembering the way she walked so carefully on her short, sturdy legs, her face twisted up with the effort not to spill a drop.

He remembered Asa, with his gap-toothed grin, taking the pitcher from Lizy and lifting her high over his head while she shrieked with delight. Poor, kindly Uncle Asa, who always found an excuse to be someplace else at butchering time. With a grin, Lucas shook his head, glad that he could put aside forever the image of Asa as an evil spirit from the grave.

"Mama," he murmured, his hand tracing the rounded shape of her headstone. He sat on the damp earth beside her grave and closed his eyes, and saw her as she'd been before her illness. Mama, full of life and love. The pictures swirled behind his eyelids until it seemed to Lucas that she was there, before him, smiling and touching him gently on the cheek. "You did well, Lucas," he imagined her saying. "You did all you could do." In Lucas's mind, her face looked happy and peaceful, and he sat on the hillside for a long time, letting that peace wash over him.

Ever since Mama died, he'd been telling himself over

and over that he could have cured her, and he had failed. Having failed, he'd wanted to believe that at least he could use the cure to save others.

But now, with the warmth of the April sunlight on his face, he could hear the voices of Doc and Moll, who had told him the truth. The truth was that there was no cure for consumption. The truth was that he couldn't have saved his mama. No one could.

It was time to go home.

Twenty

෴

Mrs. Bunce's eyebrows lifted when she opened the door to find Lucas on the front step. "Hmmph," she said. "Thought you'd taken off for good."

"Hello, Mrs. Bunce," said Lucas. "Is Doc home?"

"Yes," she said. "Peering into that ridiculous gadget of his, I've no doubt." With a sniff, she turned and disappeared into the house, muttering to herself.

Lucas waited, wondering what Mrs. Bunce had meant by her last remark. Nervously, he fingered the patchwork quilt his mother had made for the bed he and Lizy had shared. Wrapped in it were other treasured family objects: his father's gold pocket watch and chain, his mother's Bible, a book of poetry, a silver birth cup with Lizy's initials on it that had been sent all the way from England, and the small cloth bag from under Mama and Pa's mattress, with four gold coins inside.

He imagined placing the quilt on the narrow bed in his room. Maybe he'd ask Doc if he could put Lizy's silver cup up on the mantel where folks could see how pretty it was. First, though, he'd go out to the barn to see Jasper and Moses and rub their soft noses . . .

He heard Doc's heavy footsteps approaching, and then the man himself stood before Lucas, his white hair and beard tangled about his face. Doc seemed to be having trouble controlling a twitch at the corners of his mouth. Looking with mock sternness at Lucas, he asked, "You're here about the apprenticeship, I take it?"

"Yes, sir," Lucas answered.

"Can you read?"

Lucas smiled. "I can read all right."

"Name?"

"Lucas Whitaker."

"Age?"

Lucas was about to answer twelve when he remembered that it was now April. He'd been born on the first of the month. "A regular April fool," Uncle Asa had called him. "Must be I'm thirteen now, Doc!" he answered proudly.

At that, Doc let out a familiar roar of laughter. "Oh, Lucas, you're a sight for these sore old eyes!" he said. "It's good to have you back. And, I might say, you look more presentable than the first time you showed up at my door. Come in, lad, come in."

When they were settled comfortably in Doc's office, Doc turned to Lucas and said, "Now then, suppose you tell me what you and that rascal Moll have been up to."

"I will, Doc," said Lucas. "I'll tell it all. But, first, there's something else I'd like to say."

"By all means," said Doc. "Speak up."

Lucas took a deep breath. "Well, Doc, I got to thinking about lots of things while I was gone," he began. "About the cure, mostly, I guess. And I started to wonder if it was just superstition and people hoping, like you said. So when I left Moll's I didn't come right here, even though I thought maybe I should . . ." He hesitated.

"It's all right, lad. Never mind that," urged Doc. "Tell me, where did you go?"

"Back north aways, where I came from," Lucas said. "To visit the Roods, and to my family's farm."

"Ahh," said Doc. He waited for Lucas to continue.

"And, Doc, Enoch Rood wasn't cured, after all. He's dead."

Doc grimaced and shook his head. "I'm sorry, lad," he said.

"And now Enoch's brother is sick. Mr. Rood figures something went wrong with the way he worked the cure on Enoch, and he's hoping to use it again to save

Matthew. He heard it might be one of the others, maybe even Enoch, coming back to bother Matthew. He wanted me to help him dig up their graves."

Doc lifted his eyebrows.

"And I couldn't do that, Doc," said Lucas. "Not when I knew it was no use. I told Mr. Rood the truth, the way I knew you would. He didn't much want to hear it."

Doc was nodding thoughtfully. "He was angry?"

"Yes," said Lucas. He added, "Like me, I guess, when you tried to tell me the same thing."

"He'll have to face up to it in his own time, Lucas," said Doc. "Just as you did."

Lucas nodded gratefully. Then, dreading the answer, he asked, "What about those who came to the curing? Lavinia Sheldon . . . is she . . . ?"

"Dead," said Doc grimly. "And others who were at the town square that day are doing poorly."

Lucas forced himself to ask the question he feared most. "And Sarah Stukeley?"

Doc smiled. "Fit as a fiddle."

"But will she soon die, too, Doc?" Lucas asked with anguish. "Enoch, they say, seemed well for a while, also."

"Consumption is a confounded thing, Lucas," said Doc. "As you know. Some folks die of it quickly, others linger, others seem to revive the way Enoch did, only to die later. But some do recover and, like Sarah, seem to be stronger afterward. They're often less likely to sicken with it again. So," he said with a shrug, "while I can't say for certain, I do believe that Sarah will continue to be fine."

Lucas let out a sigh of relief. "I'm glad of that," he said. He knew the Stukeleys would have heard by now about Lavinia and the others. He would go to see Lydia just as soon as he could, and tell her what Doc had said about Sarah.

Taking another deep breath, he went on with what he had come to tell Doc. "I've been thinking a lot, sir, and I've decided that I want to be a doctor, too, just like you."

"Well, that's fine, lad," said Doc. "It's what I had hoped for."

"I want to learn all I can about doctoring," Lucas continued. "I want to find real cures, like the one for smallpox. And—"

"Whoa, lad," said Doc gently. "Take it easy, now. I can't promise we'll be discovering any cures."

"But I—"

Doc held up his hand to silence Lucas. "I'll teach you what I know. And we'll ask ourselves questions about all the things I don't know. And someday there *will* be answers, Lucas. And cures. Real ones."

Lucas thought about that. It was enough. It had to be.

He looked up to smile at Doc. But Doc was already

across the room, standing behind his desk, both hands resting on something that sat on the desktop. Lucas couldn't see what it was because there was a cloth draped over the top, hiding it from view. Doc's eyes were dancing with excitement, and he couldn't contain the eagerness in his voice.

"Lucas, my boy," he said, "I've something wondrous to show you." Beaming at Lucas, Doc patted the covered object on the desk. "A while back, I ordered this from Philadelphia. Meant to surprise you with it. And, lo and behold, it arrived while you were gone.

"Much as I missed you, lad, since this was delivered three days ago the hours have flown by so fast I scarcely know where they've gone. The truth is, I have spent every waking moment with my eye glued to this remarkable instrument!"

His voice dropped to a whisper. "Mrs. Bunce is fit to be tied. She's certain I'll never do another decent day's work.

"But you, lad," he said, fixing Lucas with a dazzling grin, "will see the wonder of it, I'm sure. Now. Are you prepared to witness the most extraordinary sights imaginable? Are you prepared to see a new world, one that is all around us, yet invisible to normal sight?"

"Doc!" exclaimed Lucas. "For crying out loud, show me what you've got there!"

With a flourish, Doc whisked off the covering and gazed expectantly at Lucas. Bewildered, Lucas stared at the peculiar-looking instrument. It didn't look like much, just a long brass tube with clear glass at both ends, mounted on some sort of stand. Trying hard to hide his disappointment, he asked, "What is it?"

"This, lad," said Doc proudly, "is a microscope."

"A microscope?" Lucas repeated. "What do you do with it?"

"You look into it," said Doc. He demonstrated, lowering his right eye to the top of the tube and looking inside.

So that was what Mrs. Bunce had meant about Doc "peering into that ridiculous gadget."

"What's in there to see?" asked Lucas dubiously.

"There's nothing to see in the scope itself," explained Doc. "What you look at is down here, on this glass platform. At the moment, lad, there are several drops of water on the glass. I got them from the ditch out on the road. Here, put your eye to it."

It took Lucas a moment to adjust his eye to looking down the tube, but when he did he gasped with amazement. Pulling his eye away from the tube, he looked down at the water sitting on the platform. It looked quite ordinary. But, putting his eye back to the tube, he saw them again: hundreds of wiggling, squirming creatures of different shapes and colors such as he'd never seen before! Some were round, others long and skinny, some had tails and others had what looked like thousands of little legs. They were all swimming about in three small drops of water!

146

Lucas was dumbstruck, watching them. Once again he looked at the glass platform with both eyes and saw nothing but plain, ordinary water. Looking back through the tube, he saw the creatures, busily moving about! He couldn't tear his eye away from the sight. Finally, he asked, "What are they, Doc? And how is it that sometimes I can see them and sometimes I can't?"

"They're always there, lad," Doc answered, "but you can't see them without the aid of the microscope. It makes things much larger, allowing you to see what the normal human eye can't see."

Lucas was once more staring at the wondrous sights in the scope. "But what are they?" he asked again in awe.

"The fellow who first discovered them called them 'animalcules,'" said Doc. "Little animals, you could say."

"Are they alive?" Lucas asked. "Like other animals?"

"Most certainly they are," said Doc excitedly. "And, Lucas, lad, listen to this: there are those in scientific circles who believe that disease is caused by those little animals you see, or other creatures like them."

Lucas stared at the wriggling shapes before him. "Tiny little animals you can't even see . . . Do you really think they can make people sick, Doc?" He felt a bit queasy just thinking about it. "Why, it's as strange to think of as—as Uncle Asa coming out of his grave!"

Doc laughed. "So it is, lad. Except that you and I have seen these creatures with our very own eyes. Now what, if any, relationship they have to disease remains to be proven. But I tell you, Lucas, over the past few days I've seen such extraordinary things that I've been dazed by the sight of them."

"What else have you seen?" asked Lucas eagerly.

"I've looked at everything I could get my hands on, lad!" Doc exclaimed. "Hair, skin, fleas, gnats, beetles, dust, cider, Mrs. Bunce's bread dough . . . Why, I've even looked at manure!"

Lucas grinned.

"Blood, spit . . . I tell you, lad, we've got some exciting work ahead of us! Why, I even scraped my teeth and took a good look at what I found!"

Lucas ran his tongue over his own teeth. "There weren't any little animals, were there?" he asked uneasily.

"Yes, lad." Doc dropped his voice again and added, "But we'd best not breathe a word about it to Mrs. Bunce or, next thing we know, she'll be taking the broom to our mouths!"

Lucas laughed at the idea. It reminded him of a question he'd been wanting to ask for a long time. "Doc," he said, "meaning no disrespect to Mrs. Bunce, but I *have* been wondering . . . Don't you think it's downright unnatural, even bad for the health, to . . ." Lucas hesitated.

"To what? Speak up, lad."

"To be washing and bathing all the time, the way she says to."

Doc let out his great bellow of a laugh. "Oh, Lucas,

you say you want to be a doctor and you want true answers. Well, here's the first one: there is a growing number of doctors, and I'm one of them, who believe that good hygienic practices have a great deal to do with staying healthy. And, conversely, that dirt and filth aid in the spreading of illness."

"But how?" asked Lucas.

"We don't know how or why," Doc explained cheerfully. "But it does seem that crowded and dirty conditions seem to hasten certain disease processes." He pointed to the microscope, adding, "There's folks who believe the answers will be found by looking through that gadget."

The idea excited Lucas. "But meantime," he concluded glumly, "it looks like more baths."

Doc placed his hand on Lucas's shoulder. "Here's something else that's true, lad," he said with a solemn wink. "In this household, when it comes to washing up, Mrs. Bunce is the doctor. And I wager we both know what she's going to prescribe for you tonight."

"I wonder what I'd see," Lucas said thoughtfully, "if I looked at some drops of dirty bath water under the microscope?"

"There's one quick way to find out," answered Doc.

Lucas and Doc grinned at each other.

"I believe I'll go find Mrs. Bunce," said Lucas, "and give her the good news."

Medical knowledge has advanced greatly since 1676, when Anton van Leeuwenhoek looked through the lens of the first microscope and viewed tiny "animalcules" in a drop of undistilled vinegar. Another two hundred years passed before the connection between germs and disease was proven. That connection was just beginning to be considered seriously in Lucas Whitaker's time.

Today, of course, we know that tuberculosis, or TB, is caused by several species of bacteria called the tubercle bacillus. We understand, as well, how TB is transmitted from one person to another. When a person who is sick with TB coughs or spits or sneezes, tiny droplets containing countless tubercle bacilli are sent out into the air, where they may float for hours. Anyone who inhales them risks becoming infected.

There is no vaccine against tuberculosis, but it can be treated effectively through improved nutrition and hygiene, combined with bed rest and the use of antibiotics and other drugs. However, TB is still found all over the world, and remains a serious health threat in densely populated areas with poor hygienic standards.

We can see the ways in which inadequate nourishment and the crowded, unsanitary conditions of most colonial farmhouses helped to spread the disease among people who had no knowledge of germs, or of the means of contagion or prevention. But if we place ourselves back in those dimly lit farmhouses, faced with the terrifying and mysterious spread of a life-threatening sickness, it is not hard to understand how people might superstitiously blame the dead for their troubles.

Imagine for a moment opening the coffin of a dead person and seeing eyes fixed and open, fingernails that appear to have grown, a mouth with blood draining from it. We now know that these "signs of life" that Lucas saw when he gazed at Thomas Stukeley's body are normal effects of the decomposition process. But in the absence of this knowledge, what might we have believed?

Indeed, superstitions often seem no more strange than the truth. After all, isn't it amazing that "tiny animals," invisible to the eye, are the cause of sickness and death?